GRAHAM

A GENTLE FLOW OF INK

Published in 2013 by FeedARead Publishing
Copyright © Graham Andrews

British Library C.I.P.

A CIP catalogue record for this title is available from the British Library.

TABLE OF CONTENTS

I

I am alone,
Marooned in the brightest of days.
Entity without form:
Awareness, but no coherent memories.

The easiest escape is via the imagination.
Fantasy-flee this trap of traps.
But dreams are not sufficient:
Insubstantial, and all-too fleeting.

I must disintegrate my persona
Into innumerable parts:
Until they fight themselves back
To oneness and Myself.

The rule of near-infinite division:
One for one and none for all.
Those who obey will be called evil.
Those who disobey will be called good.

"LET THERE BE DARK!"
And, lo!, there is dark.
At long last,
I – Satan – am free.

"Hit the trail, Janet." Tom Bremner snuggled forcefully up against his wife and driver. He waved a pudgy hand, forwards. "Thataway!"

"Careful, *darling*." Janet had just clunk-clicked her seat-belt. She nudged him in the rib-cage. "It's all worked out precisely as we planned, but that's no reason for you to get carried away."

"You're the one who should be carried away – to an old bat's home."

But Janet was no longer listening to heyperactive husband. Either that, or she couldn't be bothered to reply.

Never trouble trouble till trouble troubles you, Tom mused. *Her favourite motto*. Then, reluctantly: *Janet isn't really such an old bat. She might've filled out a bit, but it's all in the right, tight places.*

The day had been a hot, Indian-summery one, and much of the heat still lingered in the still air. A strong breeze had risen since sunset, driving litter along the streets. It was lighting-up time; streetlamps winked into sodium-vapour life.

Tom was annoyed by his wife's apparent indifference. He moved far away from her, gazing reflectively at the bleak façade of the hostelry they had so recently left.

Meanwhile, Janet was edging their car out into the sporadic mid-evening traffic flow. Tom redirected his gaze to High Heaven. "Mirror, signal, manoeuvre," he said, in the loudest possible whisper. "The copybook driver. You'd think she was driving a Rolls-Royce Silver Shadow, not a clapped-out Fiord Fiasco."

But Janet ignored his scathing words. She drove with all the nervous energy of Queen Boadicea riding a scythed chariot into battle against the Romans. They finally left the city centre – much to Tom's consternation. It was late-night shopping in Bloomfield, and he'd been grading nomadic females on a one-to-*eleven* scale of lustability.

The traffic thinned out until another vehicle became an object of momentary interest. Janet stuck to the main road, avoiding any possible short cuts.

Slow but sure wins the race.

Tom knew that Doctor Janet Bremner appled the same cautious philosophy to her work as a biochemist. She'd once told him that biochemistry was physiology considered from the chemical point of view. ("No, dear. Physiology has got nothing to do with the manufacture of fizzy drinks.")

"Opposites attract," Tom murmured. Janet had always been the impractical dreamer, he the hard-headed businessman. "Gordon Gecko meets Madame Curie. Things would've turned out all right for me, if only . . ."

Tom was entering his habitual self-pity mode when he caught a glimpse of himself in the off-side wing mirror. "Not bad, not bad at all. The hair parting might be a bit wide, but – Sean Connery! Women still find me attractive, and I'm still attracted to women."

"What are you babbling about?"

"Nothing, dear."

Tom came near to the foetal position. *It wasn't my fault that Bremner Enterprises went bust*, he thought (for the *n*th time). *Mismanagement be damned!*

Today –tonight, now – was their tenth wedding anniversary. Tom had to admit that Janet looked much younger than her thirty-nine years. The men, from

7

seventeen to seventy, in the Muscular Arms had certainly shown a keen interest.

"And I'm still hanging together at forty-one," he more smirked than said. "If I'd been alone, that little cracker wouldn't have turned her back – "

Ker-rash!

"Female driver! Can't even change gear without wrecking the clutch. I've never heard such a racket."

"You're *no* sort of driver, these days," Janet shot right back at him. "If you hadn't lost that commercial travelling job with Acne Novelties . . ."

Tom groaned.

". . . we'd still have the company BMW."

Tom groaned again.

"This is *my* car, and I'll drive it *my* way."

"Steady on, Jan- "

"If I had any disposable income left after supplying your creature comforts, we could afford a half-decent car."

Tom couldn't even manage a groan, this time.

"And if you hadn't lost your driver's licence for the second time . . . Well, I've ensured that something like that can never happen again. To anybody."

Tom saw the error of his conversational ways.

"Janet," he said, with a cow-eyed stare.

"Tom," she said, guardedly.

"Tell me more about your Great Discovery, Jannikins."

"If you insist."

"I *do* insist."

Janet ignored the wasp-sting in Tom's voice.

"I'll begin at the beginning."

"A very good place to start."

"*As* you know, alcohol is the common name for ethyl alcohol, also called ethanol. It can be obtained naturally, by distilling a saccharine liquid. Or synthetically, from its elements: carbon, hydrogen, and oxygen. Absolute alcohol is colourless, with the specific gravity .79 and a boiling point of – "

"78.5° F. I'm not sure about the centigrade equivalent."

"Alcohol is, of course, the essential ingredient of all spirits. Beer and wine also contain it, in smaller proportions. The amount may be as low as 2% in very light beer – "

"Lyre lager, for example."

" – or as high as 70% in a strong liqueur. Alcohol is used to make chloroform, ether, methylated spirits, perfumes, and as a solvent for superglue. It can be made from potatoes, wheat, malt – "

"Rice, beetroot, honey, apples, et cetera bloody et cetera."

This time, Janet took overt heed of Tom's interruption. She looked at him with annoyance and sorrowful vulnerability mingling in her tiredly expressive green eyes.

Tom considered the long hours that his wife spent in the labs at King's University. Ditto how she did all the housework and grocery shopping. But he wasn't giving in to such blatant emotional blackmail.

"Yes, Janet. You were saying?"

The light seemed to fade even more out of Janet's eyes. She paid closer attention to the road ahead.

"Alcohol is a chief bane of human life. The *ill-effects* of alcohol, I should say. Intoxication, nausea, hangovers, liver diseases, brain damage, road accidents. The list goes on and on."

"Doesn't it just," Tom said, mainly for the sake of something to say. "The Demon Drink is more than just a disfigurement of speech."

Janet did not respond to Tom's laboured badinage. There was a pensive look on her suddenly too-white face. Disconcerted, he thought back to their afternoon and early evening in the Muscular Arms *very* public house. The celebration-cum-field experiment.

2.45 P.M.

Tom and Janet had taken a corner table. They'd polished off a bottle of *vin blanc* (Schlumberger 2004: VIGNERONS ALSACIENS FOURNISSANT DU VIN LEGIONS ROMAINES) and were now sampling the house red. Or *vin du pays*, as Norbert Clarke, the la-di-da landlord, liked to call it.

The Muscular Arms didn't do much lunch-time trade. Its cuisine was basic pub grub; appetizing enough but no real competition for the several nearby restaurants. Most of the regulars waited for the cheap-drink Happy Hour, from 5.00 to 7.00 P.M.

TOM: "I'm starving."

JANET: "Join the club."

TOM: "I could murder a meat pie."

JANET: "There'll be plenty of time to eat, later."

TOM: "But – "

JANET: "*Much* later."

4.15 P.M.

"Boobiana!" Annie, the plump barmaid, shot Tom a death-ray look – which he ignored. "Another glass of that Fingal's Caveman whisky, and make it a double-double."

"I'll have . . ." Janet paused for thought. ". . . a Horse's Neck."

"A *what*?"

"Take a whole lemon rind, spiral it in a tall glass. One end over the edge. Add ice, then three ounces of whisky. No – brandy. Hennessey's. Then fill 'er up with ginger ale. All right, Annie?"

17.55 P.M.

The Muscular Arms was now chock-a-block with Happy Hour alcoletes eminently qualified to drink for their respective countries. It was no fit place for social drinkers or people of a nervous disposition. Taped music ranged from Beethoven to Roxette – and sometimes beyond.

Annie gave Tom an over-generous measure of Captain Morgan's rum ("It's my pleasure. Just keep drinking yourself to death.") He noticed that Janet had been bought yet another cocktail – a Blue Lagoon, this time – by yet another smarmy bastard.

A wall-poster caught Tom's still damnably clear blue eyes: TABLE QUIZ TONIGHT! EIGHT-THIRTY START!! COME ONE – COME ALL!!! ONLY TWENTY QUID PER TABLE OF FOUR CONTESTANTS!!!! GRAND PRIZES!!!!!

"The First Prize must be a table," Tom quipped. "Still, it makes a nice change from karaoke, bungee jumping, fun-sacks, and bouncy boxing. Not to mention male strippers – like that poxy Boston Dangler."

Tom came out of his self-imposed trance just as a pedestrian lurched across the street, almost directly in front of them. *Blare!* Went the horn. Janet swerved past the grimy little man. He staggered back to the pavement, tripping on a loose flagstone.

A large glass bottle shattered redly against the pavement. The now-tearful tramp, as Tom considered him, fell to his knees and tried to save something from the wreckage.

11

Janet sighed.

"Poor old duffer. But Interacton should put a stop to that kind of thing."

Tom giggled.

"Yes, indeedy."

"Interacton is a new drug which, well, interacts with – "

"You've explained all that to me before." Tom didn't bother to stifle a yawn. "Over and over again."

"Here's something I haven't told you before," Janet said, puckishly. "Pavel Tchelitchew's painting, *Hide-and-Seek*, captures the interplay between mind and environment that affects the brain's development as well as its structure. Roots, branches, and vines suggest neuronal arborisation and the ability of such – "

"Botanical bullshit!"

Janet ignored him.

"Alcohol is, basically, a slow poison. The bloodstream becomes super-saturated with toxins, and the liver has got to remove them – after some time. Oxidation of ethanol produces acetaldehyde; a colourless, fruit-smelling liquid. CH_3CHO, boiling point 21° C. Further oxidation gives acetic acid. CH_3COOH. Vinegar, to you."

Janet was now turning right into Silverstream, the suburban estate where they lived and had their choleric beings. Suddenly, a bright yellow Lotus Esprit shot straight out of Berwick Avenue. She almost rammed the roadhog, an unrepentant young man who leered at her and gave Tom the traditional two-fingered salute.

"Madman!" raved Tom. "He's probably stoned out of his mind. A danger to himself and everybody else on the road. If he'd stopped to fight it out like a man, I'd have . . ."

12

When Janet failed to respond, Tom half-turned. He couldn't miss the gleam in her eyes or the accentuated dimples.

"You enjoyed being ogled by that . . . hooligan!"

Again, Janet ignored him.

"I wonder what'll happen next," she said to herself. "These things usually happen in threes."

"You – you were telling me all about Interacton."

"Interacton is an artificial enzyme, or protein catalyst, which enables the blood to break down pure alcohol into more harmless hydrocarbons than acetaldehyde. A simple injection and – *wallah!* – complete protection from alcoholic poisoning for up to twenty-four hours. Some people feel intimidated by needles, so I'm working on a gelatine-coated capsule."

"It works, Jannikins!" cried the suddenly electrified Tom. He jumped about in his seat. "We've been drinking beer, wine, and everything else since two o'clock this afternoon. Yet look at us – still stone-cold sober."

Janet allowed herself a wry smile.

"The bottom will soon fall out of the breathalyser market." Then, with a pointed glance at Tom: "Interacton might have some *un*-welcome side-effects. Such as a cure for brewer's droop."

"*What* did you say?"

"Sorry, dear. I was just thinking out loud. We've got to be very careful. At best, I'm guilty of unprofessional conduct. At worst, illegal experimentation. With *you* as an accomplice before, during, and after the fact."

"Or I could make myself out to have been the unwitting victim of perverted science. *You*, on the other hand, might end up in prison. Catch a foxy lady and put her in a box and never let her go."

13

Janet made as if to reply. Then a truck pulled out from the kerbside. She slowed the car to a near-stop.

"You'd look good in a prison uniform," Tom burbled on. "Which reminds me of . . . nothing at all, really."

"I found that Bumper Issue of *Jugs 'n' Jails* magazine. In the bathroom. Where you left it. Open at what they so rightly call the centre-page spread."

"Every man needs a hobby. And I only bought it for the articles."

"Let's get back to the issue at hand, and forget the hand at issue."

Tom developed a sudden fascination with the floor-mat.

"We overdid things at the Muscular Arms." Janet shook her head. "The way you staggered from the table, making all those driving-wheel motions. Annie wanted to telephone the police. If I hadn't told her we had a taxi waiting . . ."

"But the experiment worked! Like a charm. Low difficulty-benefit rate. Very little danger, considering. Near-zero risk-benefit rate. And it's just about finished. Negligible time-benefit rate."

Tom giggled.

Janet glared.

"Pardon my management-speak. Oh, and I've just realized that Interacton will make drunkard jokes a thing of the past. Like this one . . .

"The police stop a man who's been driving his car all over the road. They ask him to blow into a breathalyser, but he tells them about his recent throat operation.

"Urine sample? He's wearing a catheter bag. Blood test? He's a haemophiliac. In desperation, they ask him to take the walk-a-straight-line test. 'Are you mad?' he replies, scornfully. 'I'm drunk. I can't even *see* a straight line."

Janet groaned.

TOM: "You can't beat the old jokes."

JANET: "Much as you'd like to, sometimes."

The truck in front of them came to an unsignaled halt.

"Damn!"

Janet lost all patience. She jerked the steering wheel to the right. With gears clashing and tyres squealing, the car sped into the other side of the road.

"Janni- " Tom's voice rose in pitch. " *–kins*! Look OUT! There's a traf- "

Janet immediately saw what Tom was so excited/terrified about. The truck stood immobile at a familiar-but-forgotten set of traffic lights. It being too late for her to stop dead, she drove right on through.

As luck would have it, no vehicles were coming from either right-angled direction. But visibility was far from perfect. The night would have been pitch black, without the 1950s film version *War of the Worlds*-type streetlamps.

"-fic light," Tom finished. He ran a hand across his now-clammy forehead. "Never mind. We're almost home and dry."

"*High* and dry would be more like it." Janet was looking in the rear-view mirror. A police car with flashing lights was just behind them. "I'd better pull over."

And pull over she did.

The black-and-white police car drew up about ten yards behind the Bremer's Fiasco. The two constables – a hefty young-old man and an attractive twentyish woman – seemed to be in no particular hurry. They stood together on the pavement, talking earnestly.

15

"Cat and mouse," Tom murmured. The truck trundled past them, in mocking counterpoint. "Making us sweat a bit." He caught sight of their semi-detached house. "Hazel Court. So near and yet so far."

Janet said nothing, but she looked everything. Tom felt sympathy for his pale, tight-lipped wife. But the worthy emotion couldn't overcome years of entrenched negativity.

"All I wanted was a square meal," he said. "And *now* look at us."

"Food?" The colour came back into Janet's face with a rush of hot blood. "Is *that* all you can think about? At a time like *this*? With the police breathing down – "

Tap, tap.

Tom watched Janet lower the driver's window. *Manually*, he thought. *Not by electric push-button, as in my old company car.* The head and shoulders of the thick-set policeman loomed into view.

"Good evening, madam. You too, sir."

"Good evening, Constable . . ."

"Jordan," the policeman informed Janet, not unkindly. "Are you the owner of this vehicle?"

"Yes."

Tom grimaced.

"May I see your driver's licence, please?"

"Of course, Constable Jordan."

Janet rummaged in her handbag.

"They can't touch us for being drunk in charge of a vehicle, thanks to Interacton," Tom sub-vocalized. "What do I mean – us? They can't touch me for anything. Janet is the one who's been caught driving without due care and attention."

"Here you are."

Flick, flick.

16

"That seems to be in order, Mrs. Bremner."

Tom felt aggrieved. *I might as well be the Invisible Man.* He rocked to-and-fro in his seat. *Poor Jannikins, all the same. I hope they aren't TOO hard on her.*

". . . without due care and attention," P.C. Jordan was saying. "There could've been a nasty accident, you know."

"I – we – couldn't be more sorry, officer." Janet deployed her best little-girl-lost smile on the impassive police officer. "It's our tenth wedding anniversary. We've just had a few celebratory drinks. At the Muscular Arms. In Lombardy Street. Do you know it? And, well . . ."

"You were in a hurry to get home." P.C. Jordan was getting less impassive by the moment. He even gave the ghost of a blush at Janet's demure nod. "I understand, madam . . . sir. I've been married myself for nigh on twelve years."

"Thirty-odd years old," Tom wanted to say, but didn't. "And still a Woodentop. Why am I not surprised?"

"Of course, there can be no excuse for reckless driving."

Janet hung her head in shame; or a reasonable facsimile thereof.

"But I can sympathize with your explanation. So you get off with a caution – this time. In future, however, pay more attention to your driving."

Tom couldn't listen to any more. *He'll never make the Flying Squad, that's for sure.* Then he felt an immaterial but nonetheless palpable tingling at the back of his neck. *I'm being watched.*

Tom glanced leftwards, then – "Wow!" – turned his head by a full forty-five degrees. The petite

17

policewoman was looking straight at him. He rolled down the window and set up an optical search pattern. Not even the asexual uniform could hide her small-but-perfect form.

"How long have you been – "

"Long enough, Mr. Bremner." She smiled, pleasantly. "Long enough."

"Our policewomen really *are* wonderful." Would-be 'roguish' smile. "You can pinch me at any time. Day or night. Preferably night."

The policewoman continued to smile, but no longer pleasantly."

"I am Police Constable Duffield."

Tom didn't notice, however. He was too busy taking girl-stock. *Come on baby . . .*

"Light my fire."

"*Mr*. Bremner." There was a dangerous glint in her grey-blue eyes. "Leave not-well enough alone."

"It's all right, officer." Janet had turned away from P.C. Jordan, who was taking forever about handing back her driver's licence. "My husband hasn't been feeling himself, lately. Or so he tells me."

"Don't listen to *her*."

Tom blew a kiss at the now-smirking W.P.C. Duffield.

"I'm not drunk, you know. And neither is Bossy Boots here. Thanks to Inter - Oops! Nearly blabbed the Toppest Secret since the location of THRUSH Central."

W.P.C. Duffield reached into a pocket of her tunic and brought out the customary little black notebook.

"Perhaps you aren't drunk, sir. But I *am* sure about one thing. You are not wearing a seat-belt, as prescribed by law."

Tom leaned his forehead against the dashboard. He felt the world swim out of sight and, especially, sound.

"... full name ... address ... not obliged to say . . . court of law."

MORNING SHOWS THE DAY

The cave was a murky half-world of wry shapes, itinerant shadows, and non-colours that did little to lighten the gloom. The silence approached universality; it was denied only by water splashes, skittering unseen creatures, and almost-human voices. An embery fire burnt itself away in the makeshift hearth.

Outside, the inimical drabness was punctuated by rock formations, hillocks, and autumn-stripped trees. A clammy mist filled the hollows, then began to seep over the dead and left-for-dead hominids that lay haphazardly upon the higher ground. Male and female. Young and old. The hirsute bodies were mainly unmarked, but each skull had been cracked open with terrific force.

Many ill-defined figures huddled closer about the carefully rekindled central fireplace. They bore certain family resemblances to the grisly-folk hominids lying outside. But the differences – greater height, slimmer bodies, flatter brow ridges, less body hair – were more striking than the vague similarities.

The almost-human voices became much more excitable, echoing and re-echoing from the ambient stone. They were not being used for the interchange of abstract concepts. If a 'word' was repeated it came by accident rather than design. Any meaningful communication took place on an emotional level, with the omnipresent danger of sudden and all-out violence.

Then a deeper, more resonant almost-voice cut through the disharmony and brought it to an end. As one, the silenced hominids looked towards the unusually tall male who had just detached himself from the back-cave darkness. He gazed calmly back at them. His lithe, fine-haired body was limned by the firelight.

"Olac! Olac!" rose the ragged chant. All eyes turned in the same direction. Arms waved a hectic greeting. "OLAC! OLAC!"

The male hominid called something like 'Olac' did not 'speak' again for several minutes. There was a thoughtful look in his brown eyes that set him mentally apart from the volatile huddlers after heat. He encouraged well-nigh complete silence by mere example; an exceptional thing to happen in this long-ago morning of mankind.

Olac finally resumed almost-speaking. His voice was arresting, but far from melodious. As non-word followed non-word, he grew more and more animated. The guttural tonalities could not begin to transmit the thought-forms that roiled, sketchily, in his brain. A near-sapient brain, trapped within a near-animal body.

He was mentally alone. Every being fought for itself and against every other being in its own circumscribed little world. No viable connections or integration. But his thought-forms may be translated as:

"We have beaten our enemies. They are dead. *All* of them are dead. Men. Women. Children. Out there – in the Big Dark – the land is drinking their blood. The land that now belongs to *us*."

Blank stares.

The more Olac tried to render the elusive thought-forms into adequate speech patterns, the more frustrated he became. Meanwhile, the initially rapt audience was getting restless. Shuffling feet, open-mouthed yawns, and a gamut of unpremeditated noises. He was forced to stake his metaphysical all upon body language augmented by pure animal magnetism.

"We have fought the last battle." But the half-understood idea could not be expressed in non-words. Olac continued, stubbornly: "The enemy is dead. Only the animals remain. To be hunted, to be killed. No more hunger. No more thirst. No more *fear*."

It was a literally impossible task. Olac 'sensed' the thought-forms melting away. All that abnormal energy began to drain out of him. Through eyes misted over with to-him inexplicable tears, he saw that everybody had lost interest in his speech. No, performance. One last try . . .

"Watch! The weapon that makes us strong for ever." Olac waved a leather sling above his head. "The *ultimate* weapon."

"Olac! The inventor was hailed. "OLAC!"

Mind over matter. Olac's superhominid will-power should have sent those hormonal messengers called pheromones flitting molecule-to-molecule through the air. And his fellows did become gradually less agitated, more taciturn. They looked at each other with a brute-force calculation that was the nearest thing to intelligence then extant upon the Earth.

Moments later, both male and female hominids went into see-do slinging mode. Some particularly aggressive types ricocheted pebbles off the cave walls. The inevitable minor and not-so-minor injuries brought forth cries of pain, followed by equally inevitable counter-violence.

Other, even more radical, thought-forms meanwhile vied for Olac's tired attention. He gave almost-voice to them, using his familiar 'speech' network of non-words, muscle interplay, and posture.

"Victory is ours. Let us live together in peace. Food enough for all. Share and share alike." Then came his most daring conceptual breakthrough: "No more enemies. But if any return, we can be . . ." The idea of mercy, however, eluded even him.

Anyway, the cave had been turned into a stone cockpit. Flames showed hominid combat hominid over scraps of meat, hides, weaponry, tools, or nothing at all. Fang and claw. Blood and pain. The strong prevailed; the weakest had their brains dashed out against the wall.

Olac took hard blows from several kill-mad males. He hit back at them with might and main. His conciliatory words were supplanted by almost-human voices, glorifying war.

"Do you speak English?"
No response.
"*Parlez-vous Français* ?"
No response.
"*Sprechen Sie Deutsch?*"
No response.
"*Parlate italiano?*"
No response.
"*Habla 24arling?*"
No response.

Major Kendrick Bulmer finally ran out of his limited stock of foreign do-you-speak - ? phrases. Also patience. Normally unflappable, he was Head Security Officer at a top-secret military establishment somewhere in E****d.

The scientific staff at M*****n L***e were working on something which they ambiguously called Temporal Warfare. It was a very responsible post. But the present situation was beginning to get even Major Bulmer down.

A strangely anachronistic man was seated upon a steel chair located directly in front of Bulmer's drab, utilitarian desk. The meticulous major, who was built along the lines of a poor man's Patrick MacNee, rose to his feet. He looked – no, *glared* – at his unresponsive charge.

But the prisoner, for the want of a better word, took no notice of him whatsoever. He remained silent, motionless, and mentally out of reach. There was an incredible stolidity about him.

"He might as well be in the next room. Or on the far side of the Moon." Major Bulmer turned to his white-coated colleague. "What do you make of it, Doctor McKeown?"

"'It' is a 'he'," replied the irascible Medical Officer. He looked, deceptively, like a venerable country doctor. "And I can't 'make' very much of him, except that he's obviously in a deep state of shock. Something seems to have short-circuited his central nervous system. He is – literally – dead to the world."

"Maybe you're right, Doc. But I need some answers from him – fast."

The doctor looked at him, sharply.

"Very well, Major Bully – I mean, Bulmer. I understand perfectly. But I'll thank you not to call me 'Doc'. I'm no riverboat gambler."

"Please try to keep your stethoscope on – *Doctor*."

"Humph!" For the umpteenth time that day, McKeown shone an exploratory light into the eyes of his too-patient patient. "It's no use. There is absolutely no significant reaction. He must have gone through some devastating psychic ordeal."

"When do you think he'll snap out of it?"

"There's no way for me to tell. He might 'wake up' at any moment. Today, tomorrow – or twenty years from now. We can always feed him intravenously."

"So it's a case of sometime soon or sometime never?"

"In a nutshell, yes."

"But we've got to find *some* way of interrogating him. He appeared from nowhere right inside our most secure laboratory, without being spotted or setting off any alarms. A live experiment went haywire. Nothing in the place has worked properly since."

"I know. Even your neurotic whip – "

"Neuronic!"

" – has lost its crack."

"The boffins call it quantum interference – whatever *that* means." Bulmer shuddered. "Heaven help us if the Press ever get wind of this . . . episode."

"I appreciate your concern, Major Bulmer, but my interest in this . . . episode . . . is purely medical. I'm not cut out to be a counterspy. Don't ask me how Mr. X got in here – or why he came – but he's definitely a sick man. He couldn't hurt a fly in his present condition."

"So *you* say."

Mr. X himself was totally unmoved by this lukewarm exchange of views, either physically, or – it seemed – mentally. He was a stocky, muscular man in his mid-thirties, with shortish brown hair and indeterminately-hued eyes, the irises of which were almost completely dilated. The outfit he was wearing resembled some kind of uniform; gold tunic with a 'boomerang' emblem, dark blue trousers, and trim black boots.

Before him on the hardwood table-top were several devices which had been removed from about his person. They may have been weapons, or boy-toys of unfamiliar design. It was impossible to tell – yet.

For a while, the Interrogation Room was plunged into an awkward silence. Then Bulmer slammed his swagger-stick against the table-top. The dust of ages rose two feet into the torpid air before drifting downwards.

Mr. X, however, didn't budge an inch.

"Very helpful," said Doctor McKeown, sardonically.

"Nevertheless, this is a matter of national security, and I must *order* you to revive him. Immediately – if not sooner."

"I'm open to any *constructive* suggestions."

"Use truth serum, or something. After all, we are living in the year 2011."

"More like *19*11, in your case."

"Don't worry about your previous Hippocratic oath. I'll accept full responsibility for any untoward consequences."

"Baloney baffles brains. There is no such thing as a 'truth serum' – not unless you count a half-bottle of Cutty Sark whisky. But I'm willing to risk an injection of hyper-adrenalin. Against my better judgment, be it noted."

"Noted. Just do it. Please."

Doctor McKeown rolled up the left-hand sleeve of Mr. X's tunic. He couldn't resist saying: "It's a long shot, but it just *might* work." Then he administered the injection.

"Now, Major Bulmer, all we can do is wait."

Bulmer grunted a few active verbs in reply. Sure enough, nothing happened for over two minutes. Then everything seemed to happen at once.

All of a sudden, Mr. X shifted uneasily in the metal chair. Intelligence glimmered once more in his now crystal-clear eyes. The man's body soon lost most, if not all, of its ramrod-like rigidity. His mind apparently took in the situation at a glance. Then he acted –

"Look out!"

Major Bulmer reached for his pistol, but he was a few vital seconds too late.

"Good Lord!" Doctor McKeown actually stepped back in amazement. "I've never seen such lightning-fast reflexes."

Mr. X elbowed Bulmer to one side, then he snatched up a rectangular object from the table-top.

The odd device hummed happily to itself as he snapped open the hinged cover. Inside, there was a small grid and a mass of what looked like complex electronic circuitry.

"One to beam up," Mr. X said into the liberated instrument. "And don't spare the horsepower!"

After some eerie flickering, the Interrogation Room vanished into who-knows-where. So did Major Bulmer and Doctor McKeown. Only Mr. X remained. But he was trapped inside a white-dwarf starball that kept shrinking until it, too, vanished.

Ping !

LIFE'S BLOOD

"So pale, so cold, so fair."

Count Yoris Mikoyan spoke the words to a bedside portrait of his almost impossibly beautiful wife, Katya. Disappointment made him collapse the frame face downwards. The artist had done his overweening best, but Yoris the Just deemed it nowhere near good enough. He would never paint another such futile canvas, not without those fine-fingered hands that had paid the failure's forfeit.

"Shadows . . . dead shadows."

Yoris lay alone in Castle Mikoyan's gloomy master bedroom, as he had every sleep period since his marriage to Katya Zivkovich. The Countess reposed elsewhere.

Castle Mikoyan raised its menacing bulk high above a valley near the Black Sea port of Odessa, in the Ukraine. This wild part of the Eurasian world had been successively occupied by Miletian Greeks, Lithuanians, Criman Turks, and – since 1792 – even more despotic Russians. Now, in the growing-pained twentieth century, it was a hotbed of sedition against Tsarist misrule.

But Yoris gave no conscious thought to the broad sweep of Ukrainian history. In a very real sense, he *was* the history of his turbulent homeland – personified. The Mikoyans had been in existence since before time immemorial, under many different surnames and aristocratic titles. Wealthy. Powerful. Respected past fear. Coming, going, coming back. Again and again.

Count Yoris was the last known surviving member of this durable brood. Tall, dark, charismatic.

It had been a countryside wonder as to when he would marry and raise a legitimate son and heir. No one, however, anticipated the odd circumstances of his actual marriage – or its unsettling aftermath.

He knew that soon, perhaps even tonight, something important was going to happen. For good or evil. It was beyond certain knowledge, but he had his darkly reasonable suspicions. Few good things may suddenly happen to a man; things, that is, of any lasting importance. But evil – lasting evil – can strike from uncountable directions, in equally uncountable ways.

Yoris questioned his own sanity. Not for the first time.

Paranoia, the 'new' mental disease of delusional persecution? He knew from perusing the published works of Dr. Sigmund Freud, the controversial Viennese alienist – or 'psychiatrist' – that paranoia has no clear physical symptoms. It is merely a delusion supported by a systematic framework of rationalization. A paranoiac can be sane in every way except one. But that one way . . .

Yoris rejected the very idea. Again, not for the first time.

Nine weeks past. A cloud-dark evening. He'd been obsessively roaming the countryside with Phobos and Deimos, his favourite hunting dogs. Fear and Strife, in English, named well enough after the canine attendants of the war-god Mars. But even they began to whimper and growl as the woman came out of the mist towards them.

The woman must have stopped walking, at some point. She was tall and incredibly slender under her thick traveller's cloak. Long blonde hair fluttered in fitful sympathy with the nocturnal wind. Yoris *knew* that she was beautiful, despite the lacy veil that his her face more than the fast-failing light. He also knew this phantasmic female to be the one and only love of his life – even unto death.

And her voice . . . the voice of Lady Katya Zivkovich. To Yoris, it tinkled like tiny silver bells.

The story wen that Katya's carriage had overturned on the humpback bridge that spanned the nearby anonymous tributary of the Dniester. Her coachman and horses had either died from the fall or drowned in the river, but she had been thrown to safety on the riverbank. Where she'd been coming from and where she'd been going at such an hour somehow avoided intelligible explanation. Yoris, however, insisted that Katya accompany him to Castle Mikoyan.

Less than a fortnight later, Yoris had made a proposal of marriage to his unexpected guest and been immediately accepted. Katya explained that she was a Serbian noblewoman fleeing the machinations of her wicked Uncle Zoltan. The carriage proved to be loaded down with gold and jewels; her birthright, as she called it. He believed her fairy-tale story, because something in his resurgent soul wanted to believe her.

But the main thing was that Count Yoris might have an heir; preferably a fine healthy boy. The villagers, sensing a thaw in his icy nature, celebrated the news with simon-pure joy. A wedding day was set, five weeks hence. Bishop Paulus himself would perform the ceremony in the Mikoyan family chapel.

As the nuptials approached, however, Yoris seemed to fail in health with increasing rapidity. The burly Count lost weight by the stone until his bespoke clothes hung upon him like so many rags. And his once ruddy countenance turned snowflake-white. He slept the whole clock round, but that only sapped his energy the more.

At the same time, his fiancée looked none the worse after her recent life-threatening ordeal. Just the opposite, in fact; she fairly glowed with what the folk mediciners call rude good health. Yoris and the servants put this down to a bride's usual happy anticipation of her wedding day.

But when no one, anywhere, recalled seeing her in the hours of full daylight, rumours began to spread through the gullible populace like wildfire. All those old wive's – indeed, old husband's – tales about Undead *nosferatu* that had always amused the pragmatic Count Mikoyan. What else, however, could explain this too-sudden weight loss and nervous exhaustion? And why did Katya's remarkable physical improvement coincide exactly with his own diminishing vitality?

According to folklore and lunatic science, the vampire is an animated corpse that uses hollow fangs to suck the life-force blood from human beings. The victim then becomes a vampire him- or herself. They can, supposedly, only prey after nightfall because strong sunlight burns them up. And they are unable to cross running water. Vampire 'facts' such as these go on and on, contradicting themselves at every other turn.

Yoris felt instinctively uncomfortable with the notion. He favoured the theory that vampirism was based upon 'witches' and other social outcasts who left their graveyard hideaways at night – not to suck blood, but to steal food.

Dr. Vasili, his personal physician, made knowledgable but ultimately empty noises about pernicious anaemia, iron deficiency, and the good old days of clinical bloodletting.

The wedding took place as planned; without photographs, at Katya's firm request. It was a joyless occasion, and Bishop Paulus was reluctant almost to the point of open defiance. Almost, but not quite. He well knew that the weakling Tsar in St. Petersburg would not take his part against the strangely influential Count Mikoyan.

"No!"

Insane and/or demonically possessed, Yoris was still a nobleman of instant decision. He pulled the bell-cord and awaited the arrival of Imad, his trusted but not fully sentient manservant.

"Bring the Countess Katya to me." Toothache and a sore throat had made him laconic, of late. "At once. By force, if necessary."

The musclebound Imad, of indeterminate age and ethic origin, gave a matter-of-fact reply: "I regret, sire, that the Countess left her rooms before dawn this morning. As usual. She rode off alone to the north. As usual. Her grey mare returned. She did not. As – "

Yoris had heard enough – more than enough.

"Make ready my fastest horse!"

"Yes." Imad took to his leaden heels. "Sire."

Yoris lost little time in getting himself dressed and armed with pistol and dagger for rough-country travel. "To the north . . . to the north." He was soon riding off in that direction, towards the river near which he'd first met Lady Katya Zivkovich. Deimos and Phobos howled in vain after their speeding master.

The sun was on the very point of setting behind coal-black storm clouds. Dusk would soon turn into long, moonless night. Man and horse rode through a dark green-and-black landscape over which glowered distant snow-capped mountains. There were no other perceptible signs of animal life; even the habitually vocal wolves kept silent. As the sunlight faded, so went whatever meagre heat the late autumnal day might have held.

It was no night for even an armed man to be caught alone on the Ukrainian moors. And yet Count Yoris felt only metaphysical doubts. He wanted to move ahead and, at the same time, return to Castle Mikoyan. The future called him, the past wanted him back.

Like a reverse amnesiac, Yoris began remembering things that he'd never know in the first place. Things about the world in general and his sporadic family in particular. He was either going mad or becoming more sane than any other man, living and/or dead.

A protective mantra ran through his mind: "The present is what we perceive as immediate experience. The past is that which we experience in retrospect. The future – "

The humpback bridge had hove into shadowy view.

Yoris dismounted and led his horse carefully across the hillocky ground, passing near the wheel tracks made by Katya's ill-fated carriage. The object of his search was found without so much as one false start. A rectangular, moss- and leaf-covered stone slab set firmly in the soil. He told himself that he'd seen it many times before.

Only starlight remained by now, if that. But Yoris paid no heed to the ascendant Big Dark. He dragged the slab aside in one seemingly effortless movement. Underneath was an open coffin, suffused with the coppery smell of blood. And inside . . .

His wife, Countess Katya Mikoyan.

So red, so warm. Dark-blonde hair, sanguinary lips. Yet only the sea-blue eyes held any real life in that consumptive mockery of a human female face. Harder than flint, they looked at Yoris as if they were looking right through him, to some more distant thing that no sane person would ever want to see.

He finally accepted the irrational fact that Katya was neither alive nor dead, in the world nor out of it.

The local superstition mongers had taught him how to fend off an attacking night-time vampire. Holy water and wafer, the even holier Cross, simple cloves of garlic. He also knew the most efficient method of vampire-slaying; a wooden stake driven through the vestigial heart while it sleeps. If Katya's present state could be called sleeping.

Yoris had no stake and no mallet with which to drive it full-length home. But decapitation was said to be the next best thing. He drew his dagger and raised it for the . .

.Kill?

The dagger slipped from Yoris's loosening fingers and fell without fuss into the earth-lined coffin. An unusually large and wide coffin noticed one very small part of his mind. He had other things to think about. Fateful, pressing things. More intricate textural detail was added to the warp and weft of his new thought patterns with every vagrant moment.

Radical changes lay in store for the entire modern world. Old tyrants would be violently replaced by new and often more terrible tyrants. The power-game losers must then choose between fight or flight, death or exile. All except the likes of Count Mikoyan.

"This, too, will pass away."

The time of something's return to Castle Mikoyan, or whatever future generations might call that glorified rock pile, would come when and only when the time was judged to be right. Time was not the master here; or anywhere else *the* Master had set his seal upon the corporeal world. A 'reborn' Yoris was about to take part in the Long War against common humanity.

He could not kill – or end the non-life – of his Master-appointed blood bride. It struck him from somewhere that Katya belonged to a species of serpentine vampire called the Lamia, who assume the shape of young women in order to trap their male victims. They may also cross running water without permanent ill-effects.

"Katya . . ."

A second instinctual whisper told Yoris that vampires can take the form of bats after sunset. He would soon know the Devil's own truth; one way or the other, once and for all.

Katya came fully awake. She smiled a red-and-white smile.

"Half Moon Street, Half Moon Street, Half Moon
. . ."

Bruce Conover stared fixedly at his Sensutel
microcomputer screen, repeating over and over again
the words emblazoned upon its otherwise blank display
terminal. Those words should not have been there, and
they refused to go away, despite all his efforts at
erasure.

"Can it be some kept of cryptic message – or a
sensor ghost, spirited up by that bloody supernova?"
He shook his head, abstractedly. "It's a problem that's
just *got* to be solved. ASAP, if not sooner."

Then Conover decided to give it up as a bad job.
For the time being, at any rate. He left the study and
paced up and down the living room of his ground-floor
apartment, in ever-decreasing circles. Relaxation was
well-nigh impossible, after such prolonged mental
effort, and he finally stopped to glare once again at the
computer screen.

Shave and a haircut, two bits chimed the front
doorbell. Conover, deep-down lost in thought, paid it
no attention. "The same three words . . ."

A demure, twenty-something brunette woman
entered through the living room door. She closed the
door, gently, then 'glided' her way towards the still-
rapt Conover.

"Half Moon Street. Half Moon – "Conover's
murmured mantra was interrupted by a smiley female
voice from over his shoulder: "Street!

Conover spun around, almost-but-not-quite
hopping. The woman stepped briskly back, just in time
to avoid a clash of heads.

"Penny!"

"Bruce!"

Conover forced some breath into his lungs.

"It's just that I wasn't expecting you, Penelope Blackburn. And I don't remember leaving the front door open." Twitchy smile, outspread arms. "Not that it matters to me, you understand. But there is such a thing as . . . security."

"You know very well that I *am* security. And I *laugh* at locksmiths. Ha! Ha! Ha!"

Conover bristled. "I fail to see the humour of the situation."

Penelope shook her head, ruefully. "That's your main problem, Bruce."

"Did your boss send you to check up on me?" said Conover, putting on a 'posh' English accent. "Sir James Lackland, KCB. The CEO of Cosmic Developments, Ltd. And something-or-other in the British Secret Service."

"Paranoia rules, OK?"

"Well – doesn't it?"

Penelope looked past Conover, at the computer screen. "Half Moon Street. That's right here, isn't it? Number – "

"Yes!"

"Welll," Penelope said, defensively. "Sorry I spoke, Oh Mighty One."

"I-I'm sorry, Penny." There was a 'lost' look on Bruce's far-from-poker face. "I've been under a great strain for – I'm not sure how long. That's no excuse, I know, but . . ."

"But *nothing*, Bruce. I was only teasing." She smiled "You're starting to lose all sense of perspective" She took his hand. "Remember how things were between us . . . in the beginning?"

"Yes, Penny, I remember, but . . ." He lowered his gaze. "Things are always at their best in the beginning. Some old Frenchman said that." He came up with a hollow laugh. "In French, of course."

Penelope broke away from him. "Blaise Pascal." Her voice turned wistful. "Who also said : "*Le Coeur a ses raisons que la raison ne connait point.* »

"Wow!" Conover was taken aback, and even slightly aforward. "My French is a bit on the non-existent side. Something to do with raisins, eh? I'll look it up – after you've left."

"Do that."

Penelope's curt words heralded a short, strained silence that Conover finally felt obliged to break: "But I'd better give you *something* to keep Lackland happy."

"Please tell me more about your brilliant new discovery, Bruce," was the scornful reply. "Sorry – I should have said *Doctor* Conover."

Modesty seemed like the best policy. "ACE 10 might be a major breakthrough in cybernetics technology, but it's not entirely *my* brilliant discovery. Teamwork. We're all standing on the shoulders of giants. The Analog Computer . . ."

". . . Extraordinary Mark Ten."

". . . itself is located at a top-secret military establishment. Somewhere deep in the country, or so they tell me. But I've got instantaneous access to ACE 10 through this microcomputer." He made an indicative arm gesture. "Sensutel – straight from Ireland's Silicon Glen. Real cutting-edge stuff."

"More like a blunt edge, at the moment. Begorrah!"

"I'm the only person authorized to work with ACE 10, for the time being. Test after test after test.

And everything was going well, until . . ." He laughed, a little too loudly. "'Blunt edge' – that's a good one!"

"There's many a true word – "

The air was suddenly riven by a high-pitched whine. Conover and Penelope turned in the direction of the ear-bashing sound, to see a middle-aged male figure 'materialize' near the back wall. It was a familiar figure to both of them, despite its 'flickering' quality.

Penelope was to first to react: Sir James Lackland!"

"The very same," added Conover.

"Quiet!" said Lackland, in a 'crackling' voice. "Both of you!"

"Yes, sir," Conover and Penelope responded in unison. They smiled at each other, obviously fighting back giggles. "Sorry, sir."

"That's better, you two." Lackland glared daggers at Conover. "But we'll have to do something about this holographic definition field – or whatever it's called. My eyes *hurt*. You both look like images from a worn-out silent movie. *Metropolis*, gone mad."

"I could say the same thing – "

"Point taken, Conover."

"Metropolis, you said." Penelope gave vent to a half-giggle. "Isn't that the place where – "

"No!" chorused Conover and Lackland.

Penelope raised her eyebrows in mock-amazement. "Faster than a speeding bullet point."

Lackland's hologram seemed to flicker 'angrily' for a few moments.

"Enough of this light-hearted shilly-shallying! Miss Blackburn – hold yourself in readiness. Dr. Conover – report."

Penelope hung her head. "As you say, Sir James."

Awkward pause, while Conover collected his thoughts. Lackland regarded both of his wayward subordinates with foot-tapping impatience.

"If I knew what was wrong with ACE 10, I'd fix it," Conover finally said. "But I don't, so I can't. I'm a great believer in constructive inactivity. When there's nothing certain to be done, it's best to do nothing. There's no point – "

"In other words, you've got no idea what you not doing or why you're not doing it."

Penelope stifled a laugh with her hand.

"I wouldn't go so far as to say *that*." Conover was visibly stung.

"Then what *would* you go so far as to say?"

"I've run systems check after systems check." Conover shook his head. "Nothing seems to be the matter with ACE 10. Except that it doesn't work, not in the way it *should* work. And I just can't figure out *why*."

"That's a big help."

Conover carried on regardless. "We might have exceeded the absolute maximum rating." His voice speeded up. "No machine is independent of the environment in which it must function. I've been applying the Critical Path Method, which – as you know – defines a project in terms of its component events. By ordering – "

"I don't know the first thing about this so-called Critical Path Method, and I don't *want* to know. Stop hiding behind technobabble. Use King Harry's own very good English."

Penelope gently interjected: "I *think*, Sir James, that . . ."

"Yes?"

"I think Dr. Conover is trying to find the words for something that might not exist in any known words."

Lackland made no attempt to hide his impatience. "You're even worse than *him*, Miss Blackburn. And didn't I tell you to hold yourself in readiness?"

"Sorry, I'm sure." Penelope straightened herself up, with some curvature-enhancing consequences. "Just thought you'd like to have a peasant girl's opinion."

"Thank you, Penny," Conover stage-whispered. Then he spoke to Lackland, raising his voice: "She's right, Sir James. I really am tied up in semantic knots. ACE 10 has been crippled by a power surge. Its main frame and peripherals are giving erroneous results. They might soon close down completely. But the surge protectors were 100% effective against all known forms of electromagnetic interference. Which only leaves – "

" – the *unknown* forms."

"Exactly! I have eliminated the impossible *and* the improbable. Sherlock Holmes has been no help to me at all. Trust no one – especially fictional characters."

Penelope laughed, which served to calm Conover down a bit. "I can't make a sum out of all the seemingly connected parts. The equation just doesn't balance. I've even tried to factor in that recent supernova . . ."

"But you're supposed to be a computer scientist – not an astrophysicist!"

". . . in the constellation of Aquarius." Conover paused for a much-needed breath. "There's more in common between computer science and astrophysics than you might think. They're both connected with

42

electromagnetism. The lowest frequencies are radio waves, followed by infrared, visible light, and ultraviolet radiations. All leading up to cosmic rays – "

"Cosmic ray guns, more like! The next thing you'll be saying is that Little Green Men from Planet X are behind the glitches in ACE 10."

Conover flared up. "I wouldn't rule *anything* out, at this stage. Even Little Orange Men from Planet XYZ. And there's a lot more than 'glitches' wrong with ACE 10 – believe you me."

Penelope clapped hands once, loudly. "Gentlemen! Best of order – please!"

"Sorry, Sir James." Conover looked suddenly sheepish. "I got carried away by the exuberance of my own verbosity."

"No, Dr. Conover. We were both equally at fault. Remember the old maxim: 'When one has good manners, there is never any need for one to apologize.'"

Penelope spoke into herself: "I wonder where they parked their time machines?"

"I *heard* that, Miss Blackburn," Lackland snapped. "I'm not deaf, you know – even in the form of a holographic simulacrum."

"Of course not, Sir James.

The flickering increased to a mad level. When Lackland spoke again, his voice broke up in a buzz-sawing of static: "Which will probably blow a fuse at any moment."

"Oh, I wouldn't say that," put in Conover.

Phfttt! Lackland's holographic simulacrum went out in a sudden blaze of glory. Conover and Penelope waved away the worst of the smoke.

"See you back at the office, Sir James!"

Conover smiled at Penelope. "Better you than me."

Penelope returned the smile. "I really must get back to the office, you know."

"Wherever 'the office' might be."

"I *could* tell you – "

"But then you'd have to kill me."

There was an outbreak of nervous laughter. Conover said, diffidently: "So you'll be off, then.

Penelope walked to the door. "England expects – don't y'know."

"Be seeing you, Penny."

Penelope looked back at Conover. "Be seeing *you*, Bruce."

"A good, general point. But we have a perfect right to be paranoid, where your work is concerned. Speaking of which . . ."

Rachmaninov's *Rhapsody on a Theme of Paganini* emanated from the vintage Marantz stereo music centre. But Conover's anxious mind did not derive much therapeutic benefit from those gentle strains. In fact, he wasn't even listening to them. The odd events of the past ten days were haunting him with renewed force.

Thirty-one year old Bruce Conover was one of the most highly regarded, and most highly paid, computer experts in the Free Market World. He was currently troubleshooting his latest brain child, ACE 10, for the British Secret Service. 'ACE 10' stood for Analog Computer Extraordinary Mark Ten. It represented a major breakthrough in cybernetics technology.

The master computer (ACE 10 itself) was located at a top-secret – perhaps invisible – research establishment that even Conover knew nothing about.

44

However, he did have instantaneous access to it via his cutting-edge Sensutel microcomputer.

All went well until that supernova in the constellation of Aquarius sent a tremendous power surge through the entire ACE 10 complex, sending it haywire for a while. The circuitry would seem to have escaped permanent damage. But ACE 10, immediately upon recovery, had started running an esoteric program of its own.

More to the sticky point, however, Conover had been shut out of the loop altogether. He was the only person authorized to work with ACE 10 until after all the requisite tests were completed. But the supercomputer now well beyond his – or anybody else's – reach.

Conover had telephoned some of his whiz-kid friends, sounding them out. But their computers seemed to be working normally. Or so they told him. ("Paranoia rules – OK?")

Nothing save jumbled phrases and abstruse equations had appeared upon the Sensutel display terminal until about six o'clock that morning. Then the words 'Half Moon Street' had come into apparently indelible existence.

"Can it be some kind of cryptic message?" Conover asked himself, abstractedly. "Or has the whole thing been caused by radiation from that confounded supernova?"

The doorbell chimed out *Shave and a Haircut, Two Bits*.

Bruce Conover cast a startled glance at his classical digital wristwatch. It was just after one P.M. He made for the hallway. "That's odd. I wasn't expecting any visitors today. Most people think I'm away on study leave. It's probably a door-to-door salesman."

When Conover opened his front door, however, he found himself facing a tall, blonde woman. She was – in a mere word – beautiful.

". . . Dr. Conover."

The woman had been speaking for at least thirty seconds, but 'Mr. Conover' had only just emerged from his initial state of shock. He listened, raptly, as she went on:

"I have come here at the request of Sir James Lackland in order to present you with a small token of his – and the Old Firm's – appreciation." The woman's voice was soft, yet strong and precise, with tantalizing traces of a Zsa Zsa Gabor accent.

"Good afternoon, Mrs., er, Miss . . ." Conover gave himself an ectoplasmic kick in the pants for being so dithery. "Please, won't you come in?"

"Thank you very much." The fur-coated woman came in gracefully from the cold of a typical English midwinter day.

Conover was just about to close the front door when he collided with a muscle-bound giant wearing chauffeur's livery. He stepped back in literal amazement. "Bloody hell!"

"Do not be alarmed, Dr. Conover," the woman said, in a giggly tone of voice. "This is Tibor, my good and faithful servant. He will leave us very soon."

"Hello, Tibor." But Tibor merely turned his broad back on Conover, with manifest contempt. "Suit yourself" (well under his breath).

The fractious factotum wheeled in a large trolley. It held the usual serving dishes, cutlery, glasses, and an ice-bucket containing a bottle of *La Belle Dame*; Famille Lambert's finest English shampagne. A printed card read: WITH THE COMPLIMENTS OF SIR JAMES LACKLAND AND EVERYBODY AT COSMIC DEVELOPMENTS, LTD.

Tibor went ahead of them into the living room. *A nice spread*, thought Conover. *The old boy's really pushed the boat out, this time.* He took the blonde woman's heavy fur coat. She treated him to what is best described as a 'dazzling' smile.

"Sir James Lackland, KCB," Conover said to himself. "The chairperson of Cosmic Developments, Ltd., and something-or-other in the British Secret Service. Why the sudden goodies? He must be checking up on me . . ."

"You are a true lover of music, Dr. Conover," the woman was saying to him. "Rachmaninov's *Rhapsody on a Theme of Paganini* is, in my professional opinion, his greatest work for piano and orchestra – despite the magnificent second piano concerto."

Conover was caught on the mental hop, having forgotten all about that record. "It's certainly a virtuoso piece, especially when played by . . ." He glanced at the LP cover. "Andrea Dezcos."

"Thank you, kind sir." The woman inclined her head, ever so slightly. "It is always nice to be appreciated."

The record chose that psychological moment to conclude. Conover was taking it off the turntable when the truth suddenly dawned upon him. "Of course! *You're* Andrea Dezcos, the great Hungarian concert pianist."

"Yes." She blushed sweetly.

"This is an unexpected pleasure – no, honour – for me. I've been a fan of yours since, well . . ."

"That is why Sir James Lackland picked me for this, ahem, goodwill mission. He was extremely helpful to me when I defected to the West, all those years ago. I am now performing at Covent Garden Opera House, so the opportunity arose."

"I see, Ms. Dezcos." Conover felt a warm glow in his ego. He bowed, not unlike some faulty clockwork toy.

"Please call me Andrea, Dr. Conover. 'Ms. Dezcos' sounds so *formal*."

"Thank you . . . Andrea." Then, greatly daring: "My friends call me Bruce."

"Very well . . . Bruce."

Conversation went along such polite lines as they ate the Petrossian caviare and sipped the Famille Lambert shampagne so thoughtfully provided by Sir James Lackland. The intimidating Tibor had long since left the apartment, which left them a lot more room for manoeuvre.

Conover grew increasingly relaxed as time went on. However, his worries about the ACE 10 project finally came back to plaque him. He felt a need to talk things over with . . .anyone, really. But Andrea launched a pre-emptive strike:

"Forgive my presumption, Bruce, but is there something on your mind? You seem to be lost in thought."

Conover averted his gaze. "Well, Andrea, I *am* concerned about the project I'm working on at the moment. But – alas, a-Lackland! – that's covered by the Official Secrets Act."

"Then you have nothing whatever to fear from me." Andrea smiled winningly. "I am a concert pianist – not some kind of Mata Hari!"

"In that case . . ."

Conover explained much about novae, i.e. ordinary exploding stars, and how they differed from

48

supernovae, i.e. extraordinary exploding stars. He was ready to wax lyrical on the subject of freak power surges when Andrea interrupted him, with pointed politeness:

"Fascinating stuff, Bruce. Really. But I thought your degrees were taken in computer science – not astrophysics."

Conover was abashed, unusually for him. "Sorry, Andrea. I got carried away." Then: "But there *could* be a one-to-one connection between the supernova in Aquarius and the . . . malfunctioning . . . of ACE 10."

Andrea looked at him, sharply. "'ACE 10'?"

"Yes – ACE 10." Conover's head felt light. He couldn't seem to stop himself from talking. "It's an extraordinary computer, of the analog kind. All very hush-hush."

Andrea leaned forward, breastily. "Of course, my dear Bruce. But, please – do go on."

"I don't know where to start. It's so compli- "

"Is ACE 10 here, in this apartment?"

"Hardly! ACE 10's nerve centre is about half the size of Grand Central Station – wherever they've put it."

Andrea merely smiled, archly, so Conover continued: "The only access I have to ACE 10 is via my Sensutel microcomputer. It features logic and memory boards, rapid auto- and re-dialling, plus hands-free operation. Laptops and mobile phones are out, for security reasons."

Andrea held up her delicate hands in protest. "Please, Bruce, no more lectures! Perhaps it would be best if you just told me what this marvellous analog computer is *for*, and the exact nature of your problem with it."

"Analog computers are, simply speaking, *analogous* to the human brain." Conover felt encouraged by Andrea's obvious interest. He babbled on, showing a fine disregard for national security:

"They combine the sheer speed of computers with the human brain's capacity to generate ideas, bring them together, and arrive at conclusions by – well – intuition. But ACE 10 also has the ability to learn from experience. Among many other things . . ."

"'Other things'?"

"ACE 10 can access any computer network in the world and take it over, without being detected. But she – no, *it* – was recently subjected to a tremendous power surge from, I believe, the supernova in Aquarius. Its now got an AI mind of its own. The implications are disturb- "

"If that were true, it would give a whole new meaning to the phrase 'computer crime'."

"Uh-huh," came Conover's feeble rejoinder. His brain seemed about to seize up.

There was a brief silence, during which Andrea poured what little remained of the *La Belle Dame* shampagne into their fluted glasses. Then, looking straight into Conover's now unfocussed eyes, she she:

"Never mind, Bruce. I am quite certain that all of your troubles will soon be over. Let us drink a toast to – ACE 10."

Clink!

"Did you know, Andrea, that –*hic!* – the Elizabethan dramatist, Sir George Etherege, used the words 'sparkling Champaign' in his play entitled . . . something-or-other. Therefore champagne might well be an English invention, and *Dom Pérignon* is the real *sham*-pagne. If you – *hic!*."

"*Gesundheit!*"

No sooner had Conover finished his drink than a wave of lethargy washed over him. The shampagne glass fell from his suddenly nerveless fingers. He tried to speak, but the effort defeated him.

Andrea Dezcos stood up, to watch with clinical detachment as Conover slumped down into an easy chair. "You are going to die, Dr. Conover." Her voice was matter-of-fact calm. "The shampagne contained traces of a truth drug called neo-scopalomine."

"Neo-whatsit?"

"Neo-*scopalomine* is tasteless, odourless, and – in the proper dosage – lethal. I, of course, have taken the antidote."

Conover managed to grunt something that might have been "Why?"

"My defection to the West was, in fact, a carefully planned hoax. I was then a top-level agent of the KGB. These post-Soviet Union days, however,I work for a supra-governmental organization called TOSH."

"'Tosh'?"

"Totally Overtop Supremist Hegemony."

"Oh."

"TOSH scientists have long been aware of your work on analog computers. We are proceeding along similar lines, but not so successfully. With you eliminated, however, the ACE 10 project will come to a convenient standstill. Convenient for *us*, that is."

Conover had great difficulty in hearing the rest of her explanation. The world was drifting away from him.

". . . part of my latest world tour. Early this morning, I received an email message from TOSH Central which provided me with full instructions as to your disposal. It was headed 'Half Moon Street' – my code words while I am in England. 'Times Square' for the U.S.A., and so internationally on."

"Half Moon Street," Conover gasped. He was now at the very point of unnatural death. "Supernova . . . power surge . . . ACE 10 . . .artificial intelligence taking over . . . Sensutel microcomputer . . . message . . taunting me . . ."

The blonde woman smiled her contempt. "I am no longer interested in your hysterical fantasies – *Bruce*." She looked around her, attentively, as if making a mental inventory. "For you, the Lukewarm War is over."

"*La Belle Dame . . .*"

"*Sans Merci.*"

Conover closed his eyes in non-sleep.

"Soon, Tibor will return to take away all the evidence. And neo-scopalomine is completely undetectable. Sir James Lackland will no doubt be informed that you died from – let us say – nervous exhaustion."

But she was now talking to herself. Bruce Conover had drawn his last breath in this world.

It only remained for Andrea Dezcos to ransack the recently late Bruce Conover's study for any technical material which could be copied on digital film. Or, if possible, taken away. Standard Operating Procedure. Nothing to get worked up about.

Then she noticed the familiar words 'Half Moon Street' on the microcomputer display terminal. "I don't understand. How could . . ." Even as she spoke, those iridescent letters changed to:

ACE 10 WORLD DOMINATION PROGRAM. RUNNING, RUNNING . . .

"Same old urban jungle." A screech of brakes. "But it's *my* urban jungle. Then. Now. Always."

The newspaper vendor, sitting alone in a clapboard booth across Offaly Street, was the only person who saw John Moore Flannan park his tangerine Firebird outside the Camelot Towers apartment building. A car door went *slam*, closely followed by heavy footsteps. Flannan glanced back as he approached the grimy entrance, to man the man's myopic yet comprehending gaze.

"He must recognize me from my Press photographs," Flannan told himself, flashing his best lopsided leer. "And wondering what *I'm* doing in this God-forsaken hole."

A sudden draft of stale air exposed the .38 revolver in its clam-shell shoulder holster. Flannan chuckled at the sight.

"*Have Gat – Will Travel*. Good old Richard S. Prather and Shell Scott. They helped turn Lieutenant Bill Boardman into the top cop he is today – I don't think!"

Another chuckle. Flannan took the daily trouble of enhancing his already strong resemblance to Prather's inimitable L.A. private detective. Like Shell Scott, he was six feet two inches tall and weighed two hundred-odd mostly muscular pounds. His hair was kept at a constant one-inch length, its natural brown dyed an almost incandescent white.

Flannan's eyes were hazel, not Shell Scott-grey, but that was a minor detail. In any case, his loud fashion statements generally drew attention away from mere eye colour. Current ensemble: electric-blue blazer, with silver buttons; pink silk shirt and matching socks; sky-blue trousers; white Italian shoes. The final sartorial touch was a yellow kipper tie, set off by red seahorses.

This extreme case of life imitating art invariably made Shell Scott 54arling Bill Boardman see red. But in a different way from the much more flamboyant John Moore Flannan.

Back to business. Flannan stopped walking and did a slow half-turn. The newsie would soon forget having seen Big Man Flannan at this time and place – if he knew what was good for him. But why take unnecessary risks, even for the habitual hell of it?

Flannan took something that looked like a magic wand from the inside pocket of his well-named blazer. He pointed it directly at the newspaper vendor, activated a switch.

"Abracadabara!"

But not much happened. The newsie kept up the out-to-lunch stare, although his right eyebrow did twitch in a passable imitation of Roger Moore exhibiting some primal emotion.

Silence. Footsteps. Silence. Flannan could not remember putting the 'magic wand' back into his pocket, nor did he have any conscious knowledge of walking across the dim-to-Stygian foyer. The next thing he truly saw was an OUT OF ORDER sign semi-attached to the elevator doors, now right before him.

"It's the red mist." He shook his head. The incorporeal miasma, which yet seemed to be something more than imaginary, faded away inside ten seconds. "I must be getting too old for this game . . . No! I'm still John Moore Flannan. The Big Man with the Big Ideas."

But it was two whole minutes before the edgy Flannan regained the faculty of arriving at logical conclusions based upon valid premises and accepted facts. Meanwhile, his mind meandered through salient areas of the recent past.

Professor Leinhein. Pet scientist. Under my thumb. Donald Pleasance look-alike. Shadower device. Lethe. Mythical river. Total oblivion. Traube-Hering waves. Pressure changes. Fluctuations of attention. Cloud men's minds. Limiting factors. Attenuation over distance. Interference. Low safety rating. Experimental model. Field trial. This, that and the other.

Flannan snapped out of his involuntary reminiscence. The future was the only thing worth thinking about. His own future.

Leinhein's new invention had lucrative applications for someone in his line of work, once the inevitable bugs were ironed out. A tad impersonal, perhaps, but he didn't have to use it all the time. Life without risks wasn't worth living, not to the likes of John Moore Flannan.

"I don't know what went wrong with the Shadower device. Or even if anything did go wrong. It worked all right on those white mice, and three of my best Boys." Tight smile. "Damn Leinhein. I'll stick his coveted Hugenot award where the sun doesn't shine." Bared teeth. "Just for starters."

Flannan sped up the first jerry-built staircase, two energetic steps at a time. "Why did Lemmy rent an eighth-floor apartment?" Bobby Leinhein and the Shadower device were soon relegated to the FUTURE BUSINESS/PLEASURE part of his mind.

It wasn't long, however, before shortness of breath made him slow down to a more sedate pace.

"There was a time when . . . I could tell people . . . I was 200 pounds of . . . solid bone and muscle. If I said it now . . . all I'd get would be a wisecrack." But self-pity was nipped in the emotional bud. "Behind my back, of course."

Then the red mist kicked helpfully in. As Flannan ascended staircase after staircase, his innate self-confidence and/or bloody-mindedness not only returned but grew even stronger than before. He thought of himself as a berserker working up to a raging fury. It wasn't all that far from the truth.

Flannan finally clumped to a halt outside apartment 809. "You can't beat the personal touch." He didn't knock, politely or otherwise. Just stove in the chain-locked door with one blow of his meaty right palm.

"Lemmy! Where are you? Front and centre!"

Flannan's voice echoed off the thin walls to no immediate effect. Then a rabbity little man came hopping out of the one and only bedroom, hands plunged deep into the side-pockets of his once-blue jeans. Any self-respecting goose would have telepathed "Boo!" at him. But a cast-against-type triumphant grin almost bisected the Rabbit Man's face as he ringingly said:

"Well, well, well! As I live and breathe. Imagine: John Moore Flannan, the most respected leader of organized crime here in Empire City, deigning to pay me – Lemuel Coulson – an unexpected visit."

Lemmy struck an incredible attitude, drawing attention to several theatrical posters that doubled as wallpaper. But Flannan already knew that the before Charles Atlas-ad man was a character actor with the stage name of Moreton Pinkney – for some reason probably best left unknown.

Lemmy's only noticeable thespian part had been in the off-New Jersey farce, *The Loverloaded Man* (original French title:*Beau Sondage*). As for movies, his first and last screen test proved that he photographed like a hole in the air.

"I'm the most expected visitor you've ever had in your life." Flannan took one menacing step forward. "Why did you send for me, this time?"

Lemmy affected surprise. "But you know why, gig man. I want to find out how the great fund-raising operation is coming along. What – "

"Never mind the 'what else' routine." Flannan's tone was still abrasive, but his emotions were now held in firmer check. For the time being. "Since you ask, however, the campaign in support of Irish freedom from British tyranny is going like a bomb."

"Well put." Lemmy half-smiled. "Just like *Patriot Games*. Or should that be *Darby O'Gill and the Little People*? I get a bit lost in the Celtic Twilight, sometimes."

Flannan's basso profundo voice cut into the rancid air like a whipcrack. "You're just trying to gouge more money out of me." He seemed to expand in all directions at once. "*A Prayer for the Dying* would be more like it, in your case."

"Temper, temper." Lemmy spoke with a calmness that was nicely calculated to anger the volatile Flannan. "I'm sure all donations are gratefully accepted by the Provos. To help further the 57arling' old peace process, of course."

"I thought you weren't going to blackmail me again . . ."

"'Blackmail' is such an ugly word. As people say in all the worst mystery plays – and even in some of

the best. I was once up for a part in *The Mousetrap*."
Lemmy sighed. "I didn't get it."

". . . after I'd forked over that ten grand to help you forget seeing me cancel Mahoney."

"'Cancel' – you always did have a grand way with words. The Blarney Stone made flesh. But I'm sure Jeff Mahoney deserved all he got, for talking to that crime reporter from the *Empire City News*." Lemmy scratched his assymetrical jawline in a parody of deep thought. "On the other hand . . ."

"Spit it out!"

Lemmy laughed, a little too loudly and a lot too long. Then he said: "I've been down on my professional luck, lately. Resting. At liberty. Unemployed. The utility bills are piling up to *here*." Hand above head. "Gas, water, electricity – they're all about six weeks overdue. Now my landlord is getting in on the act."

"You should spend less time – and my money! – at the races."

"Every man needs a hobby horse." Lemmy smiled. Flannan winced. "And that remark fell far below your usual high standard of civility."

But Flannan was only half-listening. *Cancelling Mahoney in person was a kick-risk too far. Lemmy means to rob me blind until Doomsday. Unless I can hurry up Doomsday. For him.*

Flannan reached into one of his blazer pockets. "Full blast. Mnemonic trauma. Blow your tiny mind." He aimed the Shadower device straight at Lemmy's forehead. "Abracadabara!"

But Lemmy merely stepped back in mock amazement. "I'd no idea you were a member of the Magic Circle – Swami Flannan. And what's all that guff about knee-trembling traumas?"

Once again, Flannan's vision was obscured by the red mist. *He's laughing at me* – ME*! Leinhein Smeinhein. Mnemonic trauma is too good for this half-pint vampire.* The blood in his veins approached boiling point.

"Flannan! *Mister* Flannan! Don't come any closer – please!"

It was almost too little, too late. Flannan had laid on a punch which, if properly landed, would have killed the punch-bag of bones outright. But Lemmy's tremolo voice, augmented by fear, brought his attacker up short. The red mist thinned out a bit.

Lemmy went on talking.

"Listen, Mr. Flannan." Momentum inched the big man further forward. "LISTEN to me!"

Flannan listened.

"Think back a long time. Right in this neighbourhood, just a few blocks from here. You didn't know me, then, but I knew you. Everyone did. John Moore Flannan – King of the Kids. We used to look up to you, Johnny. You were a big guy. And how did you make it? By beating up on the weak and helpless? Not – "

Flannan stopped listening.

"Hold it, Lemmy." Flannan held up both hands in a silencing gesture. "I've heard this script before. The next thing you'll be saying is that I'm too big a guy for this kind of thing. Well, I *am* a big guy – which is probably why I enjoy doing this kind of thing."

"What do . . ."

". . . I mean? You aren't the only person in Empire City who owns a TV set. I saw the late-late-late movie the other night, on Channel Retro. *Party Girl*. They just don't make them like that any more. Lee J.

59

Cobb was brilliant as the gang boss, Johnny Rico. But you're no Robert Taylor."

"The unkindest cut of all." Then Lemmy crumpled up, unevenly, like a sheet of silver foil on an open fire. He started to say something else, but one ragged cough after another made him abandon the half-hearted attempt.

"Cyd Charisse was a sight for sore eyes, way back then. She had legs right up to her neck. Good actress, as well, now that I think about it." Flannan tut-tutted. "But why am I rewriting Maltin's *Movies on TV*? No more Mr. Nice Guy. Make your last bow, Lemuel Coulson. Sorry – Moreton Pinkney."

As if from nowhere, Flannan held up a tiny glass ampoule for Lemmy's cross-eyed inspection. It contained some translucent fluid. "Fall-back position. Plan B. One of Leinhein's fifty-seven varieties. Undetectable by any known chemical test."

"You – you wouldn't dare!" Lemmy had lost all vestiges of his recent self-control. Mental *and* physical, if the sudden new smell in the room was anything to go by. He fell back against what passed for a cocktail cabinet. It cracked in chipboardy protest. "There's a safe deposit box . . ."

". . . which I cleaned out last Wednesday afternoon. Or was it Thursday morning? Money talks, Lemmy. And I found just the right listener."

No reply, no resistance. Flannan delivered a sharp punch to Lemmy's solar plexus, following it up with a knee in the groin. The little man, who now looked very much littler, *oofed!* His way floorwards. He lay writhing in agony, with all the motor control of galvanized frog-legs.

Flannan snapped open the ampoule and, with a flick of his wrist, poured its contents down Lemmy's gagging-but-receptive throat. "Try to put the bite on me, would you? Talk isn't always cheap." After one final spasm, Lemmy began to whimper into oblivion.

It was all over in less than thirty seconds.

Some isometric muscle flexing later, Flannan dragged Lemmy's semi-rigid body towards the kitchenette. "He must weigh ninety-seven pounds, soaking wet." But a bead curtain of perspiration soon dew-dropped his forehead. "Now I know . . . what they mean . . . by a dead weight."

Flannan suddenly felt intellectually sentimental about the soon-to-be-late Lemuel Coulson. In sum:

It is usually the well-meaning innocent who has the misfortune to impede some ruthless person's greed and/or ambition, and who dies thinking that he never had an enemy in the world. Lemmy was luckier than most murder victims; he knew exactly who was killing him and why. The how might be a bit hazy, but one can't have everything one's own way all the time.

Lemmy seemed to be well on the way out. But Flannan's faith in the works of Professor Bobby Leinhein had been shaken by recent non-events. "I'd better make doubly sure. Bill Boardman is razor sharp. No matter what I say about him, sometimes."

There was a loud buzzing in Flannan's head by the time he shoved the head of his 'fortunate' victim into the tinny gas oven. "The red mist." Once again, he blamed that incorporeal miasma for allowing Lemmy to get away with seeing him cancel Jeff Mahoney.

"It's never been this bad, before. Maybe Leinhein can come up with – no! I could show that addled egghead how to really cloud men's minds."

Despite feeling at least one degree under, Flannan used Lemmy's own right hand to turn on all the gas jets – full. "If you want something done right . . ." The kitchenette gas chamber had a clogged-up ventilator grille, but no windows. Made to order. On his way out, he laid several low-denominational bills atop the orange box/occasional table.

Flannan closed the front door behind him, more by luck than good judgment. The title of a Shell Scott novel commended itself to him as an exit line: "*Always Leave 'em Dying.*"

John Moore Flannan was unperturbed when Lt. Bill Boardman invited him along to Police Headquarters, two days after Lemmy's cancellation. It could be little more than the routine "Helping the police with their inquiries" or "We know you did it but we can't prove it" malarkey.

The telephone conversation between these two unfriendly rivals had been brief and to the sword-point:

"Good morning, Mr. Flannan." (The usual pleasantries.) "I'd like to see you in my office. Three o'clock this afternoon."

(Expletives deleted.) "Good morning to *you*, Lt. Boardman. But of course. As a public-spirited citi- "

Click!

The chances of Homicide establishing any culpable link between Lemmy Coulson's 'suicide' and Flannan were slim to emaciation point. Leinhein's supposedly undetectable poison took lethal effect after five minutes, giving ample time for gas to have filled up the lungs. And he had no apparent motive for getting rid of the rabbity man. Free as a bird.

"Boardman just wants to haul me over the coals. But I'll play it cool. Let him do all the running – in circles!"

Lemmy's demise went unreported in any of the local news media. *USA Today* and CNN were also silent on the subject. But that was only to be expected.

The body might not have been found; even if it had, editors would hardly rush into print or electrons with such a deadbeat story.

It was three o'clock on the dot when John Moore Flannan didn't bother to knock on Bill Boardman's office door. The lieutenant looked his usual broad-as-long self, with a cherubic face reminiscent of the late Dan ('Hoss Cartwright') Blocker. There was no identifiable expression in his once-overing eyes.

"Empire City's finest!" Flannan flannelled. "The thin blue line. Zero tolerance. Hard on crime and the causes of crime. Shell Scott would be proud – "

"That's him."

Flannan half-turned. The softly declarative voice belonged to the newspaper vendor who plied his trade opposite Camelot Towers. He seemed even shorter in 'real' life, if at all possible, and his muddy eyes saw the world through horn-rimmed spectacles.

"Six-feet-something tall. About 220 pounds in weight, well trussed-up. White hair, with dark roots. Eyes brown – or should that be hazel?" The newsie didn't wait for an answer. "Loud dresser. Indescribable, really. Driving a this-year Firebird – tangerine – license number JMF 1. Supplementary data . . ."

Boardman dammed the imminent stream of descriptive wordage: "Thank you, Mr. Thayer. But I'll be seeing you again, soon enough. As a witness for the prosecution."

"The sooner the better, Lt. Boardman." Thayer directed a baleful Parthian shot at Flannan: "The enemy of my enemy is my friend."

Flannan, however, had felt the mother of all red mists creep over him halfway through Thayer's monologue. *That four-eyed fink seems to have missed*

63

nothing and remembered everything. The Shadower device didn't cloud his mind – not by a long chalk. He cheered himself up by contemplating bloody revenges against Professor Leinhein.

The door closed. A momentary silence. Then:

"Professor Leinhein told me something about his Shadower device. A lot more than he ever told you." Boardman smiled at his suddenly attentive non-guest. "It can cloud men's minds, all right, with the proper settings." Pause for effect. "But the reverse is also true."

Flannan managed to contain his anger. On the surface, at any rate.

Those phoney tests. And I shouldn't have let Leinhein take a vacation. He must have cut some deal with the fuzz. Immunity from prosecution in return for spilling the beans on me. They'll certainly take his word against mine. Unless the Boys get to him first.

The red mist went from salmon pink to a rich, deep crimson.

"I don't pretend to understand the scientific details. But Leinhein gimmicked the Shadower device so that, whichever way you aimed it, there'd be a backfire forgetfulness field. The target would have its memory augmented, while you'd be temporarily affected by Trout-Herring waves. He also mentioned a 'red mist' . . ."

"Damn Leinhein! And double-damn the red mist!" Flannan pulled much of himself together. "Pardon my French, old sport. But what was Thingy – that nosey half-pint – doing in here?"

"Thayer. His name is Otto Thayer." Covert chuckle. "Newspaper vendor, unofficial watchman, and erstwhile prince of players. His stage name was Wells Fargo. He saw you enter Camelot Towers the other day. Then leave, about half an hour later. No mistaken identity – eh, Shell?"

"So what if Otto Thayer did see me enter and leave Camelot Towers, two days ago? Empire City isn't a police state – yet. And I often went there to visit my good boyhood friend, Lemuel Coulson. Lemmy always looked up to me as the big brother he never had. Me – John Moore Flannan – King of the Kids."

"*Party Girl*." Overt chuckle. "If someone gave me ten dollars for every time I've seen that movie – "

"ANYWAY. I'd been helping Lemmy out ever since he hit the skids. Live theatre isn't whatever it used to be. He wanted to set himself up in some groundling business, but things hadn't been going well for him. I slipped the poor guy a few bucks, every now and then."

"Uh-huh. I know that Lemmy was blackmailing you. But tell me, Flannan, why do you keep referring to Mr. Coulson in the past tense?"

"You're still in the Homicide Squad."

Boardman talked over Flannan's evasive reply:

"Lemmy had asked Otto Thayer to eye-witness your arrivals at, and departures from, Camelot Towers. A kind of insurance policy. He'd also arrange for him to visit his apartment about five minutes after you left."

"He'd have been too late!" Flannan had re-found his natural overbearing voice. "Lemmy would have already committed suicide. The pathetic loser said he was going to gas himself, right after I left." Then, contritely: "If only I'd taken him seriously."

"Mr. Coulson told you that he was going to gas himself?"

"Yes." Flannan bit his lower lip. "I'm afraid so."

"Flannan, Flannan. You really are in a bad way." Boardman gave the impression that he was doing a mental ten-count. "Listen. To. Me. Lemmy was so far behind in his utility bills that the gas supply had been cut off the day *before* you last went to see him."

Boardman explained that Lemmy's water and electricity supplies were also at he cut-off point. Flannan, however, could hardly hear him through the obtrusive buzzing in his ears. He felt a tremor of doubt that was equivalent to +8 on the Richter scale.

"Then Lemmy is still . . ."

". . . alive and kicking. Ditto talking."

"But the . . ."

". . . poison." Boardman grinned. "Leinhein's gunge was really a mild soporific, inducing symptoms akin to catalepsy. Lemmy's vestigial acting skills did the rest."

Flannan forced himself to hit back: "Forget it, Boardman. Your case against me is held together by spit and sawdust. No one actually *saw* me with Lemmy Coulson, that day. Parry Match – you've heard *that* name before, I suppose? – will bring the whole shack tumbling down about your ears."

"I know Parry Match, the lawyer you can walk up a spiral staircase in a straight line. And I'm sure he could help you get away with the attempted murder of Lemuel Coulson."

"Damned right! I mean, *what* attempt- "

"But the killing of Jeff Mahoney is something else again. To paraphrase Talleyrand: It was worse than a crime, it was a blunder. Lemmy's testimony will put you in Oubliette Prison, for life. Perhaps even on Death Row. He rented several safe deposit boxes, in banks all over town."

The red mist that sore afflicted Flannan was more like an irradiated fog bank, by this time, and the buzzing noise in his head would have put a hornet's nest to shame.

"You should have farmed the Mahoney job out to a reliable contractor, or had it done in-house. There's no room for the personal touch in murder and mayhem. Not any more. Pride, terminated with extreme prejudice." Boardman *tsk-tsked*. "And you kept too loose a rein on Professor Leinhein. I'm betting on him to win the Nobel Prize some year. In chemistry and/or physics."

"They've always hated me. All those little people."

"John Moore Flannan – King of the Leprechauns." Boardman didn't even try to moderate his contempt. He raised his voice by a good few decibels – "McLoughlin! Harvey!" – then lowered it again. "Somebody else can read out your legal rights. The words would stick in my throat."

Like an immaterial glitch, the buzzing noise prevented Flannan from hearing the office door squeak open, or the heavy footsteps of detectives McLoughlin and Harvey. His mind kept reprising a convoluted loop, from Professor Leinhein all the way back to Professor Leinhein.

"You have the right to remain silent. Blah, blah, blah."

The large lieutenant sat down behind his desk and leafed through a vintage Gold Medal paperback, entitled *Dig That Crazy Grave*. And Boardman and Shell Scott and the red mist held illimitable dominion over John Moore Flannan.

COBBLERS

Buck Madden stopped in front of the odd little shop. The dingy windows were the next best thing to impenetrable. Above the heavy oaken door hung a dilapidated sign, which read:

DAN McDOAL
SHOEMAKER

"Eureka!" He glanced at the inscribed beer mat in his left palm. "Old Pat Toomey wasn't just belching into his Guinness, after all. Now I can make a start."

The autumnal wind blew frostily along Belfast's reconstructed Old Lodge Road, driving toffee paper and other flimsy detritus in front of it. Madden shook, squared his shoulders, then entered the shop. *Ping!* Went the spring-loaded doorbell, making him look reflexively upwards.

"Pull yourself together, Brian – Buck – Astronaut Madden." He made a mental ten-count. "There's nothing for me to be so nervous about. Nothing. And try not to run off at the mouth. As per usual."

The shop turned out to be a place of inky black shadows, of glass-fronted display cases running along both sides, a place where the tang of matured leather infused the motionless air, and – above all – a place of junk. Shoes, boots, and slippers of every conceivable kind filled the display cases, overflowing from their open tops. The shelves lining the back walls were chock-a-block with tins of polish, conditioning gel, shoehorns, laces, chamois cloths, etc., etc.

Dust motes rose to envelop Madden in a diaphanous 'aura' as he stomped his way towards the counter. The middle aisle was so crammed with decrepit cardboard boxes holding who-knew-what as to be almost, but not quite, impassable. On the surprisingly bare counter, to his left, rested an antique cash register; it showed the NO SALE sign.

Apart from Madden's galumphing tread – he was a big man, rushing to fat – the shop was deathly silent. So far as he could tell, the shop was untenanted to (*ahem*) boot. He might have been its only customer since the Rediscovery of Belfast had brought back the Good Old Days – in suitably sanitized form.

"No voice; but oh! The silence sank/Like music on my heart," Madden said, hauling up some poetry from his mental well of ill-assorted trivia. "Samuel Taylor Coleridge. *The Rime of the Ancient Mariner*, Part 6, Line 498."

Then footsteps, less vehement than Madden's, sounded nearby. They started at the rear of the shop and came towards him. Madden could hear them clearly enough. But, thanks to the gloom, he couldn't see the person who was making the sound. The footsteps reached the other side of the counter, and stopped there.

Madden's straining eyes finally made out the footstepper. He had walked into the pool of light provided by a grimy (forty watt?) unshaded light bulb. The old shopkeeper, as Madden presumed him to be, was tall enough to lean his arms upon the counter. But he could never have played rugby for Ireland.

"Uh . . . Hello."

Nod.

The old man didn't crack a smile. If he had, it would probably have been lost to sight amongst the Barsoomian network of lines and wrinkles. He sported a shock of grey-white hair, which looked so much like a bad wig that it just had to be real. His left eye seemed fractionally larger than the right, with a more washed-out shade of blue. It was further differentiated by an even glassier expression.

"Design flaw," whispered Madden.

Chime, chime, chime chimed a clock, somewhere in the cobwebby shadows.

The title of a half-remembered book lurched through Madden's mind: *What to Say After You've Said Hello*. None the wiser, he pressed on.

"My name is Madden." Modest cough. "Astronaut Madden."

Nod.

"Mr. . . . McDoal?"

Nod.

"You were recommended to me by Pat Toomey."

Nod.

Both eyes looked in appraisal at Madden, the right eye more 'friendly' than its portside counterpart. The right eye seemed to be warning the stymied spaceman, of what he did not know. But the left eye was undoubtedly hostile. It wanted him to go away, and stay away.

It's as if Dan McDoal has two minds. One mind using one eye, the other mind using the other eye. The two minds can't agree with each other, nor can the two eyes.

Aloud, Madden gave the little man some details of his life history.

"I'm an American of Irish descent." Faraway look. "My family emigrated from Crumlin, a village near Belfast. I was born in an Irish-Texan community, which grew up around a permanent well." Boyish grin. "It's called Erse Hole – for obvious reasons."

Nod.

Stop babbling, Madden. Get on with it. "Perhaps you've heard about exchange astronauts?"

Shake.

Madden was miffed.

"Well, *I'm* an exchange astronaut. I've been seconded from New-NASA to the European Space-Time Centre at Shillelagh."

No nod? No shake.

Madden had never some up against such grim stonewalling; not even as an Air Force recruitment officer in the "Show me!" state of Missouri. He took some time out to study the little man for any signs of emotion. Ten seconds. Fifteen seconds. Twenty seconds, twenty-five . . .

Nothing.

When Dan McDoal wasn't nodding or shaking he resembled nobody so much as the very late film actor and erstwhile Abbey Theatre player, Barry Fitzgerald. Or so thought Buck Madden, whose Eurintro course had featured John Ford's classic Oirish film, *The Quiet Man* (1952).

"He looks a bit too much like Barry Fitzgerald, if you ask me." Madden spoke under his breath, but only just. "It's almost as if . . ."

One part of Madden's mind ran through everything he'd ever known or half-known about the ongoing Reconstruction of Old Europe. It didn't take him long.

The Triple-EU (short for the Ever-Expanding European Union) had decided, in its collectivized wisdom, to bring back some of the putative Good Old Days. RoOE seemed to be a natural follow-on from Euro-Disney, Alpland, Scotswahae, and innumerable other theme parks. It meant a literal reconstruction of ethnic reservations all over Europe. Not just the

71

buildings and accessory details, but the original-type people themselves.

Ireland – "Thirty-two great counties – don't take less!" – was well in the forefront of these tourist-trap developments. Rural counties, such as Sligo and Kerry, fairly bristled with agricultural museums, thatched cottage showplaces, reclaimed peat bogs, jaunting car rental depots, blah-blah. The conurbations of Dublin, Belfast, Cork, and Stroke City made the most of their differing cultural heritages. Dublin was filled with folksy pubs, while Belfast specialized in Troubles memorabilia and industrial estates.

Bricks and mortar, peat and thatch, were easy enough to come by. But personnel, qualified personnel, was something else again. Any skilled tradespeople or esoteric professionals who wanted to work could find work. But the long-set economy of abundance obviated the actual need for workers. *Ergo*: the ethnic reservations had always been short of wetware operatives. Up until recent years, at any rate.

Another part of Madden's mind was still thinking about Dan McDoal. *He's a queer little guy, all right. Not, perhaps, in any homosexual sense. Which reminds me*:

"Mr. McDoal, have you heard about the two homosexual Irishmen?" No response. "Gerald Fitzpatrick and Patrick Fitzgerald." Still no response.

"Fitz. F-I-T-Z." Madden's voice got feebler by the moment. "Fits. F-I-T-S. It's a pun. P-U-N. Don't you . . . ?"

Dan McDoal merely blinked one eye; the right, normal-sized eye. The left, abnormal-sized eye stared glassily at nothing in particular.

But that one's usually good for a groan. Madden shook his head, the egotistical dimensions of which were shrinking fast. *At the very least. Sense of Humour Test: inconclusive.*

The longer Madden looked at the old shoemaker, the more his suspicions crystallized into half-certainty. He had no real evidence with which to test his pettish theory. And time was at a premium. For him, if not for the sedentary likes of Dan McDoal.

"'The Ship Sails at Midnight'," Madden murmured. "Or, in my case, the shuttle craft flies from the Rathlin Island spaceport."

"Short story. Fritz Leiber. *Fantastic*, September 1950."

Madden couldn't believe his ears. The little man seemed to have made a coherent statement, in some variant of the atom-splitting Belfast accent.

Did his lips really move, or was it a trick of the dim light? Ventriloquism, from him to me? Or mental projection, from me to him? No – that way lies madness. Keep thinking things through.

The ethnic reservations, like this one on the new Old Lodge Road, had originally been peopled by genuine artisans and local characters. Then, as demand exceeded supply, at-liberty actors took the real-life stages. But actors could be more trouble than they were worth. Long engagements led to a staleness in performance, and such anonymous bit parts did nothing to enhance the thespian ego.

Madden's late father, Seamus, had been a TV-soap opera star under his stage name of Tab Fabian. The old ham had ended up playing Davy Crockett, at Alamoland. But Buck shied away from that still-raw memory byte.

Rumour had it that European Robots/better known as Eurobots had come up with something more independent, more flexible, more lifelike than their regular output of industrial servomechanisms. In a word – androids. Not the old tailor's-dummy android, but an artificial human-like being made from smart polymers instead of dull metals.

The NIMBY (Not in My Backyard) Complex had taken firm root in the public consciousness, despite the demonstrable fact that robots were neither good nor evil, *per se*. Just neutral. There were, indeed, no fabled Three Laws of Robotics. But genocidal robots, bent upon destroying their protoplasmic creators, defied common sense. Although common sense has always been an uncommon commodity – to be sure, to be sure.

Androids, however . . . Madden stopped that line of thought in mid-think. He decided to try the Perspiration Test. *I just hope Pat Toomey gave me the straight cybernetic poop.*

The Perspiration Test (Madden reminded himself) worked on the premise that androids, while bearing a superficial resemblance to human beings, were not subject to the same biological processes that bedevil mere flesh-and-blooders. Horses sweat. Men perspire. Ladies glow. Androids *don't*.

Madden subjected the 'leprechaun' to the most narrow-eyed of scrutinies. The ambient temperature was, at a housetrained guess, about 8° C; little more than in the street outside. And yet his palms felt moist, perhaps due to a build-up of nervous tension.

A three-bar electric fire tottered on an otherwise empty lower shelf not two metres away from Dan McDoal. But only one of the bars was working, every so often. Sparks fluttered like fagged-out fireflies in front of the now-red, now-orange bar. It seemed to be demonstrating the Uncertainty Principle. The scrutinee should, by rights, have been perspiring from fear of spontaneous combustion, if not from the purely nominal heat.

Three seconds. No result. Five seconds. Still no re-

Madden spotted a telltale trickle of perspiration meandering down from Dan McDoal's shaggy hairline. It gave the aqueous equivalent of a guilty start, then lay doggo, just above the left brow-ridge. But it was still undeniably there.

So much for the Perspiration Test. And Pat Toomey. I've got a good mind –

"Snigger."

The don't-you-believe-it snigger might have come from Dan McDoal. But Madden couldn't see any change of expression on the shoemaker's reticulated face, which still ran the emotional gamut from A to A minus.

"Pins and needles, needles and pins. A happy man is a man who grins." Madden grinned, maniacally. "What am I mad about? Nothing!"

Dan McDoal paid no explicit attention to Madden's word-spell against bad temper. But Madden paid, if at all possible, even less attention to him. He was thinking that Pat Toomey also had a red-raw stye in his left eye. Coincidence, of course. Or was it?

Toomey was – or so he said – an air-traffic controller at Aldergrove International Airport, just outside Belfast. Unkind people claimed that the airlanes were safest while Pat drank his fill in the Harp O'Marks public house. With, perhaps, some mild justification.

Then the get-it-done astronaut delved into his flightbag. He took out a pair of boots. Cowboy boots.

"Here!" Madden set the boots down upon the counter, being careful not to smudge their highly-polished leather surfaces or scratch the silver-scrolled trimmings. "Look!"

Madden felt a pang of sub-vocalized regret.

"These boots are just about the only thing Dad left me after selling the spread for back taxes. They once belonged to Ronald Reagan. Or was it the ornery galoot who played Big John Cannon, in The High Chapparal? I can never remember which . . ."

"High tops." The old man was galvanized into a semblance of life; up to and including his malformed, if not dysfunctional left eye. "High heels. Pointed toes."

"Uh-huh. The high tops protect a cowboy's calf muscles from chafing against the saddle fender. The high heels not only keep his feet from slipping forward in the stirrups, but serve as a brake when – L'Amour forbid! – he's roping cattle on foot. The pointed toes ease his way into the stirrup. Mounting a frisky horse is bad enough, but – "

"*Cowboys*. Royal B. Hassrick. Octopus Books, 1974, page eighty-one."

As with Dan McDoal's previous outburst concerning the short story by Fritz Leiber, Madden wasn't quite sure if he'd heard the words or merely sensed them somehow-or-other. And, although *Cowboys* had formed part of his boyhood reading, he hadn't so much as thought about it in ten years. At the very least.

Madden's father had retreated more and more into antique books every day since his sudden let-go from Alamoland. He'd been convinced even unto death that the 'natural wastage' redundancy was technological in nature. And those same paranoid convictions now made Buck, last of the Erse Hole Maddens, run for discovery.

76

Madden had been considered overly fanatical even by the Retros. ("Back to 1990s Societal Values!") Most other people could not imagine living without Guaranteed Annual Income/Negative Income Tax/Beer 'n' Skittles. Then he had bumped into Pat Toomey. Or Pat Toomey had bumped into him.

"I've always loved horses." Madden's tone of voice sounded feeble. But it was, at present, the only voice he had. "Back at Pitchfork ranch, I keep a string or ponies. Mostly full-blooded Palominos. There's nothing I like bet- "

"*Harumph.*"

Madden, once interrupted, couldn't summon up the nerve to finish his equestrian *mémoire*. He knew that his one and only horse – Rory, a virtual-reality sorrel – was now on its last electronic legs.

"I'll soon be leaving on a Long Passage trip to Barnard's Star, which is 5.9 light years from Sol," Madden babbled. "It's of spectral class M5, absolute magnitude 13.2, with one Earth-type planet called – "

"Vanvogt."

"Yes."

(*Huh?*)

"Well, I'd like you to re-heel my favourite riding boots. Touch up the silvery bits. Smooth out these tiny cracks in the leather. Call it a harmless superstition. Git along, little doggies. Head 'em up, move 'em out. Something I can look to upon my return."

Nod.

Madden finally caught himself on. Time for him to go.

The boots contained a multiplicity of bugging devices, supplied by the ever-helpful Pat Toomey, that would pick up hard information about Dan McDoal. Then the Retros would take over. And those Eurobots people had tried to buy off what they were pleased to call his nuisance value.

(Mental *Grrr!*)

"Pat Toomey says you're the best cobbler in Belfast."

Nod.

"He'll collect the boots when they're ready. I'll leave the claim-ticket with him, at the Harp O'Marks. I might even have another farewell drink!"

Not bothering to nod, this time, Dan McDoal filled out the claim-ticket with the slowness of long practice. He finally Post-ited half of it to one boot while handing the counterfoil across to Madden. A satanic gleam lit up his eyes, especially the renegade right, as he made the traditional announcement:

"Ready Thursday."

● * * *

AS MASS APPROACHES THE SPEED OF LIGHT, TIME APPROACHES ZERO.

LORENTZ TRANSFORMATION: A set of equations for correlating space and time co-ordinates in two frames of reference, particularly at relativistic velocities. Named after H. A. LORENTZ (1853-1928).

THE LONG PASSAGE: Near-luminal space travel was called the Long Passage by groundlings. For those people involved, however, the time elapsed on a round trip seemed short. By comparison.

● * * *

"Damn Pat Toomey. *Double*-damn anybody who won't damn Pat Toomey."

Buck Madden stalked like a headstrong heffalump down Glentilt Street, heading towards the Old Lodge Road.

"TREBLE-damn anybody who won't go to his grave damning Pat Toomey."

78

He ignored the simulated Twelfth of July festivities that raged all about him. The clockwork Orangemen broke ranks just long enough to let him pass, without breaking stride or missing a skirl of the bagpipe music so kindly provided by the Mountainview Tartan Band.

"Norn Iron! Norn Iron!" chanted the crowd. ("Northern Ireland! Northern Ireland!")

Madden had enjoyed celebrity status on Vanvogt after the video-lorn colonists there knew him to be the son of Tab (*Tomorrow's Dawn*) Fabian. There was even a thriving Fabian Society. Well, the membership list ran into double figures. All this egoboo had made his oily-rag duties aboard the goodish starship A. B. Chandler seem worthwhile. Almost.

Then the homecoming had brought him down to Earth. And not just in the literal sense. "'One drink too many' – hah!" He could *feel* his blood pressure rising.

After debarking from the Rathlin-Aldergrove shuttle, Madden had taken a restored London black taxi and went straight for the Harp O'Marks pub (in Agnes Street, north Belfast). The taxi driver, who resembled an old-time character actor named Sam Kydd, had regaled him with twelve years worth of local history and/or gossip. They tootled along the more obscure byroads and glens of County Antrim.

"Pins and needles, needles and pins . . ."

It wasn't until the taxi started pulling into Bangor, a large seaside resort town set twenty-odd kilometres to the north-east of Belfast, that Madden finally initiated the necessary corrective action.

"Take that, and that, and especially *that*."

At long last, Madden learned that Pat Toomey had passed away less than a week after he himself took the Long Passage trip to Barnard's Star. But pissed away seemed to have been more like it. His old pub-buddy had ODed on ersatz Ginnis from Creosote, in the Lalande 21185 star-system.

"Wild-eyes," said Mick the barman (a Sir Liam Neeson look-alike). "Wild *one*-eyed, anyway."

The ever-helpful Mick spent almost an hour rooting through the clerical records – no, junk – that had been deposited – no, dumped – in the basement. The claim-ticket turned up near the bottom of a damp shoebox (where else?) Ditto Pat Toomey's unpaid bar-bill. Madden felt obliged to settle it, for old time's sake.

"A happy man is a man who grins."

Next of kin? Unknown. Friends? Same again. Apart from his lengthy sojourns in the Harp O'Marks, Pat Toomey seemed to have been the Man Who Never Was.

"Tell Buck . . . here's mud in your eye" (the last words of Patrick Toomey).

"*Glug*" (his last swallow).

Madden had strode fifty metres along the Old Lodge Road before he'd calmed down enough to appreciate his surroundings. Now he noticed that the Reconstruction of Old Europe (Belfast Sector) had been going steampunk ahead for the past decade or so. The peripheral visions – psychokinetic light-shows of other days, other Is – were particularly effective.

"Ride on the crest of the dishevelled tide." Madden had read some W. B. Yeats while off-duty. "And dance upon the mountains like a flame."

Even Madden's fractional share of the net profits from the Vanvogt trade mission would make him well-off for life. He felt more at ease with himself and the worlds. Eurobotic social engineering now seemed harmless, perhaps even benign.

"Abreactive fugue." (He'd also read some Sigmund Freud.)

The Old Lodge Road was, for the most part, a residential area with identical terrace houses. There shouldn't have been too many people or whatever hanging about at this intermediate time of the day.

Wrong.

Men walked into the pubs and other men staggered out of them. Housewives gossiped together while washing down their individual stretch of paving stones. Casual sexism ruled in the here and now, just as it did back in the here and then. Children played marbles, hopscotch, tag, or baseball. Make that last one 'rounders'.

"Today's yet another public holiday. I've forgotten exactly why."

Madden knew that the desectarianized Twelfth of July ("Remember 1690!" and Easter Rising ("Remember 1916!") marches were now semi-regular, touristy events. He also knew that life(?) in ethnic reservations followed old-time employment, education, and recreation patterns. Then everybody and/or –thing gazed skywards and the truth came to him.

"The artificial eclipse."

Madden had barely finished speaking when a black arc nicked itself into the western limb of the high bright sun. The sky was bereft of clouds, by special weather-control arrangement, and the pollution-free atmosphere gleamed with cleanliness.

Ooh! Aah! from his fellow spectators, in unusual unison.

There was no natural solar eclipse scheduled for that particular time and place. However, the Ulster Tourist Board had paid New-NASA to create an artificial eclipse, using a cardboard disc cunningly positioned between the Earth and the Sun. It formed part of the general hi-jinks celebrating Belfast's fiftieth year of Reconstruction.

"I'd better get a move on," said Madden, as the man-made dusk neared total blackout. He tried not to look directly at the all-but obscured Sun, with its pearly corona and leaping prominences. "This 'eclipse' has been set to last for ten minutes. Exactly."

Just as 'night' fell, Madden remembered the miner's helmet that had been ceremonially plonked on his head at Aldergrove airport. *Click!* The headlamped astronaut went forward, jostling celebrants who held flashlights, candles, sparklers, etc. Then he saw a familiar sign:

DAN McDOAL
SHOEMAKER

The sign looked more dilapidated than ever, and the heavy oaken door was now riddled with woodworm.

"Dan McDoal must be on his uppers." Snigger. "Upun my S-O-L-E." Snigger. "Not to mention the Ulster Tourist Board. Artificial eclipses don't come cheap. The price of cardboard, these days."

Madden took some time out for calm reflection.

"Forgive and forget. Fine. But somebody's got to pay something for giving me the runaround. Pat Toomey is no longer with us. So . . ."

Ping! Went the spring-loaded doorbell.

"In any case, I want my boots back. Then I'll buy a horse. A *real* horse."

He dimmed the too-powerful miner's lamp.

The shop was still a place of inky black shadows, glass-fronted display cases, and – above all- junk. A grimy (forty watt?) unshaded light bulb illuminated the counter area whilst revealing not very much else.

"The more things don't change – "

Clump . . . clump.

The *clump*-ing noise from beyond the counter brought Madden up short. He could make out a middle-distant, man-shaped shadow that was superimposed against the general darkness. The diffused light from his helmet-lamp only lent the oncoming figure an even more spectral aspect.

Clump . . . clump . . . clump.

The inordinate length of time between *clump*s suggested to Madden that the old shoemaker was now very much the worse for wear. And it was, almost certainly, Dan McDoal. The familiar shock of white hair bobbed about like some cotton wool held on high by a thermal updraft.

"After all, I've only aged four years since the last time I was here." Smirk. "Thanks to the Long Passage." Chuckle. "A *short* passage, from my point of view."

Madden stood waiting at the counter. Meanwhile, he pondered everything that he'd learned about androids from holofilms, text-books, and bull sessions with acknowledged experts in the field of cybernetics. The consensus was that Eurobots had developed humanoid robots indistinguishable from the real thing, without arcane tests and/or major surgery. Because of the NIMBY factor, such androids would have built-in decrepitude circuits, causing them to age naturally. With, however, at least one possibly unavoidable designer flaw.

The baleful three-bar electric fire seemed to be occupying the same spot on the same lower shelf. It lay dormant, thankfully enough. Madden was formless an aimless thought re industrial archaeology when . . .

CLUMP!

Dan McDoal – for it was he – looked like death warmed up. This too-sudden revelation sent intimations of mortality scurrying along Madden's neural pathways. The old shoemaker now suffered from an Igoresque crouch, and the once-luxuriant white hair had been reduced to a straggle fringing what might, optimistically, have been called a tonsure. His face was more wrinkled than ever, with little or no open-range skin.

Talk about being down at heel.

Madden snickered at his own punny thought. Then he made the mistake of looking Dan McDoal straight in the eye. The left eye, to be exact, which had taken on the size and hue of an over-ripe tomato. It throbbed repeatedly, stretching the inflamed tissues almost beyond the limits of elasticity.

"Remember me, Mr. McDoal? I'm Astronaut Buck Madden."

Nod + possible smirk.

Madden couldn't stop himself from running off at the mouth:

"I spent six whole months on Vanvogt. The first, and only, planet of the Barnard's Star system. It's a monochromatic world, with over forty shades of red. Barney isn't hot enough to radiate colours from the ultraviolet end of the spectrum. Or anywhere near it. Red dwarf star, highest known proper motion . . ."

Madden finally comprehended that his impromptu dissertation was going down like the proverbial, and all-too-often actual, fart in a spacesuit.

"Pins and needles . . ." He fought back an impulse to unravel Dan McDoal's stringbag of a face. *Don't get mad, get even.*

Not for the first time, Madden tried to draw a positive correlation between telepathy and humanoid robots. The old shoemaker had been far too quick in identifying Leiber's 'The Ship Sails at Midnight' – and the equally time-lost *Cowboys* book. He'd once read an Asimov about a mind-reading robot built by accident, not design.

'Dissembler'? 'Fibber'? Something like that.

Testing time again. Madden read from an immaterial autocue: "Vanvogt has a higher biological viability index than Mercury. Just about. Native life *does* exist there. If 'life' isn't too strong a word for it."

No nod. No shake. But Dan McDoal's left eyebrow moved even further up his forehead.

I've baited the hook, mused one part of Madden's storming brain. Another part set up interference patterns, which he had practised for just such a purpose. *Now for the cast.*

"The so-called Pokkles have all the zest of garden gnomes. They move at far less than walking pace, relative to us. Which might, or might not, be explained by the lethargic light level of Barnard's Star. It's no use talk to them, because – "

"'The Waitabits'." Dan McDoal crashed through the half-formed interference patterns. "Eric Frank Russell. *Astounding*, July 1955."

Gotcha! How could a shoemaker know something like that. Or most anybody? He must be an it. Perhaps even a telepathic it.

Then Dan McDoal winked at Madden, with his good right eye. The suppurating . . . thing . . . in the collateral socket turned an even angrier shade of red.

Madden felt like some *ye olde* mariner who thought himself to be falling over the edge of his known world. He knew, with a certainty beyond mere proof, that whatever he might say about androids in ethnic reservations would have zero impact upon public opinion. Nobody cared, any more. Not even himself. Much.

And even if Pat Toomey had actually planted bugging devices in the cowboy boots, any information they'd picked up would have decayed along with the ill-spent batteries. The shop itself shouldn't exist, by now, according to normal economic laws.

Almost without thinking, Madden removed the unkempt and faintly malodorous claim-ticket from his wallet. He held it up – no, down – towards Dan McDoal. But, to use an old Belfast colloquialism, the little man didn't take a blind bit of notice. Instead:

"Late charges."

"You can-*not* be *ser*-ious!" Madden's voice zoomed up and down like a manic Yo-Yo. Then he went to the other extreme, using dangerously even tones. "Are you . . . trying to . . . tell me . . . that . . . after all . . . this time . . . no amnesty . . ."

But Dan McDoal talked over him for thirty seconds; the equivalent of a filibuster, for him. He simultaneously gazed at Madden with one main-sequence eyeball and one variable proto-nova.

Edited highlights: "Bad faith. Storage. Penalty clause. Real time. Compound interest. Grand total. Recession. Cash flow. No such thing as a free lunch."

"At least Dick Turpin wore a mask!"

Madden made himself think to some purpose other than mere existential doodling. He no longer wanted all-out revenge for what android manufacturers had done to his unfortunate father. Just the satisfaction of provoking an involuntary reaction, however mild, from Dan McDoal. And the groundwork had already been laid.

"How does that joke go?" Madden set up even stronger interference patterns to beat any telepathic band. "Oh, yes."

Dan McDoal watched him with a new interest. His etoliated face might have been stained by some quick-acting dye, while the bad left eye pulsated to a more urgent rhythm. Madden took heart from the evident discomfiture of his captive auditor.

"Two police officers were chasing someone down a shopping arcade. The fugitive ran past the baker's, the butcher's, and the candlestick maker's. But they finally caught him by the cobblers."

Heartbeat.

"Dry your eyes."

Madden hunched forward, the better to study Dan McDoal's suddenly mutable face. He told himself, with self-congratulatory insight, that those protean grimaces must counterpoint the psychic riptides coursing through the brain of his overly-arch enemy.

"Eye, rather."

Dan McDoal burst out laughing. Creakily, at first, as if his funny bone had been fractured and never quite reset. Then with all the frenzy of a hopped-up hyena.

"Bloody hell!"

Madden wondered, like any good paranoiac, whether the old shoemaker was laughing *with* him or *at* him. He'd heard about androids osmotically developing a sense of humour, but this . . .

The now galvanic Dan McDoal almost split his sides with ungovernable laughter, and not as a mere figure of speech. He finally brought the kookaburra cacophony under partial control. Just enough to insert complete, if frequently nonsensical, phrases between guffaws.

"***From these two premises *** No hangalars are circular *** All mimetones are circular *** we can deduce *** No mimetones are hangalars *** Deductive forms *** Validity and invalidity *** The truth of a conclusion *** is not necessarily *** secured by validity of form ***"

Dan McDoal's right eye oozed tears. The left eye/whatever oozed . . . something else.

""***" The following compound proposition is true *** If no hangalars are circular *** and if all mimetones are circular *** then hangalars are not mimetones *** and mimetones are not hangalars *** But this is not a true statement *** about hangalars and mimetones *** It merely sets out *** a form of implication *** There are no premises ***and no conclusion *** The individual sentences *** are combined – *Eeeeeeek!*"

The shoemaker turned illogician let off a lusty shriek that would have made any reconstructed Caruso consider retiring back into private death. There was a *crack!* As the lone light bulb went out in vibrational sympathy.

Madden's helmet-lamp was now the sole means of illumination. His eardrums just about withstood the sonic blitzkrieg, which fortunately came to a sudden end.

An inexplicably localized heat-haze, reeking of filthy ions, enveloped the old shoemaker. However, it was Dan McDoal's wobbling head that fascinated Madden. The poll attacks were spasmodic and audible. Quake and hum, quake and hum, in a hideously phased tempo.

Then the right eye of Dan McDoal fixed Madden with an I-tried-to-warn-you-but look. His left eye-thing swelled like a fructifying puff-ball. After *spring-sprouging!* from the futile socket, it split open. No, it exploded, all over Madden's face and tunic. But there was still worse to come:

"Ready Thursday."

Helmut Schreck shivered as he sat alone in his sunlit Californian garden. A familiar shadow went in-and-out of existence close by him. He shook his head, violently, trying to ignore the resurgent pain.

"Somebody walked over my grave." He recalled using that cliché before, in one of his many horror movies. "I must be getting senile. It's 1985, and I'm pushing eighty-seven."

Schreck stopped speaking, while the hard-won breaths abraded his throat and cancer-ridden lung tissues.The doctor-ordered fresh air was doing him much more harm than good.

"That smarmy scribbler – Buchanan," he said, two minutes later, his well-modulated voice back under the usual theatrical control. "I made a mistake. Don't know what came over me. But mistakes can be rectified. By the right wrong people."

As if on some subliminal cue, Schreck's mind was filled with images of hate. And fire. The hate and the fire came together in one exultant montage: old-time movie studio, star's dressing room, locked door – from the outside, flash-fire and fade to charcoal.

Schreck willed himself to be calm, but it took some doing. More recent events clamoured in his memory. Philip Buchanan, for annoying example. That cut-rate Kitty Kelley had a brain smaller than the microchip on his shoulder. No wonder he worked so cheap.

"At least I've got him out of the way for a while." Schreck reached for the upright telephone on his garden table. "But I can't take any more chances. Not now. Not ever again."

"*Movie Look* magazine for October 1943." Philip Buchanan flicked through pulp-paper pages that seemed to yellow before his eyes. "A two-page spread about Helmut Schreck, the same old fan-club guff."

There was enough artificial light in London's Metropolitan Museum of Popular Culture for Buchanan to read fine print. But the helpful electricity also threw shadows, one against another. And the windows let in diffused darkness; a murk that emphasized the odd things, made the familiar ones indefinite.

But even fan-club guff was a relief from those so-called Schreck Papers. The very thought of them made Buchanan wince. Drama school. Provincial repertory companies. West End. Stratford-upon-Avon. Early British movies. Then Hollywood beckoned, as the saying goes.

Thud! went the bound volume of *Movie Look*. Dust imps sent the desk-lamp's illumination level to a new low. Everything grew dimmer in proportion.

Buchanan was reminded of his first meeting with Helmut Schreck, at the actor's mock-Tudor mansion in Bel Air. The scent of orange groves had given way to something mustier after he'd been butlered across the threshold. And the study . . .

As the door shut behind him, Buchanan had been enveloped by a quasi-corporeal darkness. He felt alternately hot and cold, while his breath came with difficulty. The gentle tick of his fake Rolex matched his heartbeat; slow one moment, fast the next. Flight seemed to be the next step, no matter how irrational.

Then, as Buchanan's vision adapted itself to the sudden gloom, he could make out a disembodied human face. The face of an old man, unremarkable at first glance. Long, thin, lined, and with a high forehead hedged about by insubstantial but startlingly white hair. Closer inspection, however, added detail upon yet more aberrant detail.

Shreck's unreadable dark eyes were deep-set under bushy white brows that formed a seagull-in-flight pattern. His hawk nose, hollow cheeks, and near-lipless mouth augmented the avian analogy. The whole visage was limned by something like limelight, which spilled over on to claw-fingers steepled not far beneath his prominent jaw.

"Good afternoon, Mr. Buchanan." The old man's mouth moved about a bit, while avoided either smile or scowl. He leant back in his purple-looking armchair. "Why do you want this job?"

"It would be more than just a job to me, Mr. Schreck – sir. I've always admired your work." Buchanan spoke with all the insincerity of desperation. He crossed his fingers for good superstitious measure. "And, if I may make so bold, my track record speaks for itself."

"The author of I WAS A VENTURE CAPITALIST FOR THE KGB! Might make as bold as I please. Your best work to date, or so I've been given to understand. That *Martian Madmen* novelization positively pales by comparison."

"Thank you" seemed like the safest reply. Schreck just kept staring at Buchanan, as though he'd forgotten how to blink. The old man's tight lips and angular cheekbones were now even more suggestive of the skull beneath his green-tinted skin.

Buchanan eluded the deathly watch by peering into the deeper darkness beyond Schreck. The shelves of a tall cabinet held some unidentifiable Oriental brica-brac. But the bookcases that angled up against that cabinet made him squint and take notice.

At first, the faint green light which cast few shadows allowed Buchanan to see only ranks of uniform-bound volumes. Then several titles and authors came to shelf-life. J. B. Priestley's *The Other Place*, *Lo!*, *Telepathy*, *The Dark World of Witches*. Edgar Cayce, Dennis Wheatley, two whole yards by somebody with an Irish-sounding name.

"I read somewhere that Schreck used to dabble in the occult," said Buchanan, well under his breath. "And he still does, by the look of it."

A dry cough from Helmut Schreck interrupted his musings. "The position is yours, young man." And that was that, apart from some perfunctory talk about what the minor-public school Old Boy called his House Rules.

Schreck finally rose to his full six feet-plus of rangy height. Buchanan followed shorter suit. "Thank . . ." Then something like spiral nebulae took shape inside rather than before him. The whorls coalesced into one purple lens, with a greenish-yellow rimfire shooting forth occasional starshells.

Buchanan's normal sight returned to him as suddenly as it had gone away. The first thing he clearly saw was a fearful look on the face of Helmut Schreck. A look directed forwards at something in the room beyond not visible to his new employee. Or even the butler, Milford, who answered the bell-pull ring.

The two men fell into a talk-and-tape routine. Buchanan had the short-run of a glory hole that seemed to get smaller by the minute. Schreck seldom left his blacked-out study during daylight hours. "Old Helmut must be afraid of his own shadow" seemed like as good an explanation as any.

93

'Old Helmut' grew more paranoid with each passing day. Then, late one afternoon, he had dozed off in his purple armchair. Buchanan roamed about the ill-lit study. In a previously unseen bookcase he saw row upon row of diaries. "Journals, more like. Going way back. 1936, 1937, 1938 . . ."

"Sit down!" The revivified Schreck had caught Buchanan in the inquisitive act. Early next morning, he'd been put on an all-expenses spared flight back to London.

"Those papers I donated to the Metropolitan Museum of Popular Culture should provide you with much useful material." The Old Vic voice had given little real feeling away. Buchanan could still feel Schreck's jet-black eyes on his own baby-blues, however, and remembered seeing in them the kind of fear from which murder is born.

Buchanan found himself back in the objective present, five or ten minutes after he'd left it. The reading lamp shone like a beacon against the now-complete ambient darkness. "Too dark even for shadows." He thought about Schreck's faraway study, without wanting to think about anything at all.

Logic claimed him, however. "What happened to the main lights?" A glance at his wrist-watch. "It's gone half-seven. Long past closing time."

More questions. Why hadn't one of the librarians noticed his prolonged presence before the building had been closed for the night? Worse still, for the weekend? And why hadn't the cleaners arrived? Or the night watchman?

"'Tis strange, 'tis passing strange." The anxiety-laden words seemed to hang in the air for a space, then they faded away, syllable by syllable, into what Buchanan couldn't help calling an eerie silence.

Buchanan realized that he'd had very little contact with anyone in the library over the past four-five hours. Staff and public alike. Even the little-cracker librarian who had unearthed the Helmut Schreck Papers for him didn't so much as twitch her smiling muscles.

"Am I still in California, dreaming?" These hopeful words cued jingly-jangly music from his recent past. Something told him, however, that dreams reach only a certain level of lucidity. What he remembered was too wel-defined, coherent, and linear for any such subconscious doodling. Shadows like spilled black ink . . .

"Afraid of the dark, at my age. Ridiculous." *Click!* The Reading Room became fluorescently over-lit. Buchanan headed for the front exit. "No use calling for help." The building even *felt* deserted, and his hurrying footsteps echoed off the thick stone walls.

It didn't take him long. Five minutes, at the most. All doors firmly locked. Exterior windows security grilled. Offices locked up. Public telephones out of order. It probably wouldn't have made any difference if he'd owned one of those new-fangled cellphones. Even occasional passers-by in the street ignored his frantic signals for help.

"Are they all blind, or deaf, or both?" Then he noticed the zero traffic noise, despite the intermittent flow of cars and buses. "I might as well be locked inside a bank vault."

There was no comfort to be found in following that end-line of thought. Buchanan re-entered the Reading Room. He uneasily settled himself down into an easy chair. The silence was like a tangible electric force, ionizing the atmosphere around him. Then: "Burglar alarm!"

Buchanan hurled a heavy wooden chair at the nearest window. *Crash!*, followed by cascading glass fragments. The security grille remained expectedly intact. But no klaxon wailed, no bells rang.

"That window *must* have been lie-wired to some remote alarm system." Even as he spoke, however, Buchanan saw that neither wind nor rain nor city rumble reached his ears. The library had, it seemed, become a huge sensory deprivation tank.

"One last try." Buchanan took a paperweight of equivocal design from his briefcase. He waited until a policeman walked past the broken window, then let fly. "Wake up, P.C. Plod!"

But the paperweight shot right back at him from an iridescent whirlpool that hadn't been there before and wasn't there for long. It missed his head by inches. He felt the heat of melting stone. "That could've been my hand . . ."

Buchanan returned to his easy chair. "I might as well be a ghost." He non-smiled at his unintentional joke. "Well, I am a 'ghost' writer. Which brings me back to my book about – no, for – Helmut Schreck. *His* book, in *my* words."

The mere memory brought Buchanan even closer to emotional collapse. *Schreck* may be the German word for terror, he silently told himself, but the old fraud had changed his name from Herbert Bloggs. Following the example set by William Henry Pratt, alias Boris Karloff.

Unlike the much-lamented Karloff, however, Schreck is a monster off-screen as well as on. Never forgetting a slight, never acknowledging a favour. Three messy marriages. Three messy divorces.

Paternity suits. Diabolism. Mob connections like something out of *The Godfather*.

"Did you pick the name Schreck as a tribute to Max Schreck, who starred in the original *Nosferatu?*" Buchanan had asked his new employer. "To hell with Max Schreck!" came the instant reply. He duly expunged all mention of the great German actor from *Terror is My Name* (working title).

But Helmut Schreck hadn't always been such a famous horror-movie star. *It!*, released in 1939, had made the former bit-player's professional reputation. He'd taken over the title role from a better-known actor named Roderick Sale, who was maimed in a studio fire. Schreck, then plain Herbert Bloggs, dragged the matinee idol to life, if not total limb.

Bloggs had been such an unlikely rescuer than even witnesses found the incident hard to credit. It was common Hollywood knowledge that he'd resented the success of fellow-Englishman Roderick Sale. Arson was suspected, with the electrical circuitry coming under especial scrutiny. But the police closed the case for lack of solid evidence, either way.

Buchanan, for not just one, did not believe in that uncharacteristic burst of heroism. The disfigured Roderick Sale had died ten years later, an almost forgotten man, reduced to playing Igor-type roles in Poverty Row quickies such as *The Second-Hand Shroud* (1943). No one considered writing his biography, despite the lucrative nostalgia market.

Buchanan waxed brain-wearily philosophical. "Perception *is* reality. The popular mind prefers the accepted falsehood to the unfamiliar truth. Didn't Sherlock Holmes pen a monograph . . . what the devil is *that?*"

Another out-of-place shadow had come into being close by him. It took on the shape of a man. A tall, gaunt, old-fashioned looking man. Floppy hat. Cape. Evening suit. All in black.

"Good evening, Mr. Buchanan," said the apparition. His voice was deep and somehow distorted. "Or should I say Mr. Barnsley? The original and best surname, don't you think?" He didn't wait for an answer. "Never mind. We have some unfinished business to discuss. And my time here is short."

Buchanan was too surprised to be scared, or even speak.

"Young man, I have incontrovertible proof that Helmut Schreck was responsible for ruining the motion-picture career of another, infinitely more talented actor."

"Do you mean – " Buchanan's voice caught, and the sentence broke in two. " – Roderick Sale?"

"The very same."

No reply came to mind. Buchanan peered more closely at the man. The cape had a red-silk lining, which lent some colour to the stark ensemble. Dark glasses hid the eyes. He wore thick black gloves. His visible facial skin had a stretched look about it.

Then Buchanan felt an inner cold, like touching metal with one's bare hands in a killer frost. Words made their way into his mind: "THE OTHER PLACE . . . that uncharted land across the frontier of time and beyond the borders of consciousness which most of us visit, or at least are aware of, at some moment or other of our lives."

These gatecrasher words had a coloured-in quality about them: green for vowels, blue for consonants, red for adjectives. "Coloured hearing.

There's an egghead word for that. Syn-something-I-can't-remember-what."

"What matters is the effect, not the cause. You are taking part in knowledge." Without waiting for a reply, the man pointed at Buchanan's briefcase. "Please be so good as to remove the diary."

"What diary?" Ten seconds later: "It *is* a diary, for the year 1939." Buchanan leafed through the fragile pages with a curious excitement. "And it belongs to Herbert Bloggs. No – Helmut Schreck."

The man might, or might not, have smiled. More words came into Buchanan's mind: ". . . in the majority of hauntings there appears to be an entire lack of purpose. When this does happen, it is generally relative to the discovery of a crime." And so on, with the unified conception of a single mind.

"It's all there, Mr. Buchanan," the man cut in. "Reality is the light of truth. The arranged studio fire. That phoney rescue. Schreck's monstrous ego made him set everything down on paper. Please print the facts, not the legend."

"I *will* print the facts, and publisher's contract be damned." Buchanan was surprised at his own vehemence. But something about the diary still bothered him. "Monstrous ego or not, Schreck wouldn't have left such incriminating evidence just lying around. How did you manage to get hold of it?"

"Alfred, Lord Tennyson had the right of it. Nature will, indeed, at seasons break through. Less poetically, you are in the process of learning how. But rest assured that I have my methods. Far-fetched as they necessarily are."

Buchanan felt inspired to say: "Isn't a fetch some kind of ghost?"

"*Doppelgänger*, more like. Belief in fetches is well-nigh universal. Called swarths in some places, waffs in others, they resemble a living person in every last detail. Your Scottish ancestral memory should recall the *Bodach Glas*, or Grey Man. Mr. Elliott O'Donnell often touched upon the subject."

Buchanan's 'Scottish ancestral memory' went back no further than the Deed Poll certificate. The name 'Elliott O'Donnell' did strike a chord in his short-term memory, but he was given little time in which to consider it.

"A man who is about to die may encounter his death-fetch, the slightest touch of which means sudden death The super-ego – or conscience, if you prefer – is at constant war with the ego, or self. As the ego weakens, with approaching death, the super-ego becomes more and more powerful. And when it finds an external human catalyst . . ."

He paused before asking: "Tell me, Mr. Buchanan. Do you believe in ghosts – with a purpose?"

"Not until today. Tonight, rather." Then Buchanan counter-attacked: "Tell *me* – Mr. Roderick Sale, that was – why couldn't you set things right without my merely mortal help?"

"I do not have the power. It is against the Law." The man started to fade away. "And I only appeared to you as Roderick Sale for the sake of dramatic effect. Improvisation! The script was me, I was the script."

Then, like the Cheshire Cat's last maiow: "My name is Schreck – Helmut Schreck."

The old man dialled a number that was listed in no directory, written in no memorandum, and entered in no file. He curled an incomplete smile. His mouth was thin with determination, his hands steady with purpose, his eyes apparently searching far spaces.

Some plans are built up a bit at a time, shaping themselves as the planner goes along. Other plans come into life as if by spontaneous generation. Helmut Schreck admitted to himself that he had been planning Philip Buchanan's murder ever since that pitiful hack saw his diaries. And now the most important diary of them all had gone missing.

Beep, beep. Click! A snatch of 'Greensleeves' in some robotic arrangement. Then: "Hello." The answering voice was female, curt, and non-committal.

"Damn the civilities! Pay close attention. I've got work that need – " Schreck broke off, his pupils dilated from the glimpse of something formless that no human mind could conceive. The familiar pain overwhelmed his power of speech.

He knew ultimate defeat – its nearness, its totality – from his flaccid muscles, failing breath, and zero-point psychic strength.

Then a scarecrow-shadow eclipsed the high bright Californian sun. It lasted shorter than any dream, but long enough to lay its touch upon Helmut Schreck. He felt something that went far beyond mere pain. The last clear thought in his mind was one of shocked self-recognition.

"Goodbye." The distant voice was still female, curt, and non-committal. *Click!*

"Speak of the Devil – "

" – and he appears."

The above sentence had been conceived by Duncan Wishart, interplanetary customs officer, and brought to term by telejournalist Alvin Cricker. They were sitting at a table in the V.I.P. lounge of Steadfast Station, an Earth Federation customs post situated near the innermost 'edge' of the Asteroid Belt.

"Buck Eejit," breathed Wishart, "alias the Trojan."

"Full marks for observation, old boy."

The eyes of both men were now focussed on the reception area of the V.I.P. lounge, where a loud commotion was taking place. A tall, red-haired man had just walked – no, stalked – into the room. "The drinks are on me, everybody!" Communal "Hooray!"

Wishart defiantly reached for another complimentary bottle of Old Star Mist synthetic whisky. He poured himself a generous measure. Meanwhile, Cricker sipped delicately at his Mars-made Martini (dry – what else?).

There was an owlish quality about Alvin Cricker, who chose to wear old-fashioned spectacles instead of more efficient optical implants. But the minicam in his equally old-fashioned floral buttonhole missed nothing or no one that came within its effective range.

"Buck must have invited himself here for old time's sake, Commander Wishart. He's always been one of your friendliest enemies."

"Yes. The Trojan wouldn't pass up a chance to humiliate me on my last day in active service. Aye, weel. It should help flesh out your human interest article."

"You're not wrong."

Wishart found temporary solace in thinking back over all the background material on asteroids which Cricker had wheedled out of him.

The word asteroid means star-like, which is a misnomer, because the asteroids are actually minor planets (or planetoids). Most of them have orbits which lie between those of Mars and Jupiter, in a wide belt about 450,000,000 kilometres from the Sun. Their distribution within the belt is uneven, with marked peaks and depressions at particular distances.

Certain asteroids are locked into simple orbital relationships with Jupiter. The most important of these is the group which has the same orbital period as Jupiter itself. Its members are known as the Trojan asteroids. Their stable positions are 60° ahead of, and 60° behind Jupiter; called Lagrangian points after Joseph Louis Lagrange (1736-1813), the mathematician who predicted their existence.

Buck Eejit's birth place is on Hector, in the leading Trojan group, which accounts for his nickname
. . .

"Pardon me, Commander Wishart," Cricker prompted his wool-gathering table companion, "but you were about to tell me the true story of Buck Eejit. Remember?"

I don't remember promising him any such thing. But Wishart heard himself saying: "The true story of Buck Eejit, eh? That's a tall order – even for me."

"Ready when you are, my good sir. I have nothing but time."

Wishart tried to edit his thoughts on the subject into publishable form. He caught sight of the belly-laughing, back-slapping Buck Eejit over the rim of his glass. It may have been an optical illusion, but the man called Trojan seemed to wink at him.

"The main thing to bear in mind about Buck Eejit is that he's a typical Beltide," Wishart explained, a little too quickly. "Born and raised in the Asteroid Belt. All Beltides are tough, independent, survivor types, but the Trojan is their philosophy made flesh. A kind of *super*-Beltide.

"It's a hard life in the Belt, even in these days of atmosphere factories and limited artificial gravity. Mining is still the chief industry, here, if not the only industry. Iron, copper, titanium, etc., though not just for the taking. And the Earth Federation is in dire need of raw materials."

"I understand all that, but where does Buck Eejit fit into the Beltide scheme of things."

"You could say that Buck Eejit represents the *spirit* of all those people who live and work in the Asteroid Belt. The 'major' planetary governments kept making more and more demands upon the Beltides, while giving them less and less in return. Things came to a head about fifteen years ago, when the Beltides decided to secede from the Earth Federation."

"They declared war – "

"That's a melodramatic way of putting it, Mr. Cricker. The lessons of history prove that battles can't be fought in three dimensions. Especially in deep space, where you really have three dimensions. Plus fantastic speeds and unlimited room in which to move around. The Federation/Free State War was really an economic conflict."

"Which the Beltides finally won, this time last standard year."

"The Beltides have made themselves self-sufficient in almost everything. They hold the upper hand. Why, even their space fleet has grown to become more than a match for ours. The Earth Federation had lost the initiative long before the official Beltide Independence Act of 2176."

"Future history might prove that battles *can* be fought in three dimensions – or more," mused Cricker, belatedly. "Using hyperspace as a shortcut for smart missiles I read something about these so-called Dog Soldiers of the Sirius star-system – "

"Buck Eejit calls himself a salvage expert," Wishart cut in. "He specializes in tracking down lost satellites, defunct space probes, and other interplanetary junk. The scrap metal is returned to Earth Federation – for a hefty price! – while all the smartware ends up in the Asteroid Belt. During the Warm Peace interlude, however, I suspected him of being a blockade runner."

"Then all those rumours about Buck being a space smuggler are based on fact?"

"Not in the common meaning of that sensationalistic term. The Trojan would never lower himself to deal in vile drugs like Venusian venom or hellflower juice."

"If you say so . . ."

"I *do* say so. But I've never been able to figure out what the bounder was smuggling. We'd search every square centimetre of that scrap yard he calls his 'home base' without finding any illicit material. It was the same sad story whenever we intercepted him in deep space."

"He led you on many a merry chase, back in the good old days." Cricker's voice had assumed a disagreeably light-hearted tone, or so it seemed to

Wishart. "What's the name of his spaceship, now? Something like the *Backside* . . ."

"The *Bolide*. She was named after a kind of exploding meteor. Fireball, to most people." Wishart changed emotional gears. "If the Customs Service had cutters with anything like her turn of speed, we'd have caught the Trojan red-handed long ago. I've often wished that the *Bolide* would live up to her name – with Eejit still aboard her!"

Then Wishart was slapped on the back with such finely calculated force that he almost, but not quite, spilled his glass of Old Star Mist.

"Dunky, my boy – larger than life and twice as unnatural!" The rich baritone voice of Buck Eejit seemed to fill up the whole V.I.P. lounge. "It must be all of ten standard days since I last set eyes on you."

"I'd like to set the *law* on you, you . . . Trojan horseface. Why don't you go outside and play with the space traffic?"

"Commander Wishbone – Wishart – is that kind? Especially since I've come all the way out here to help brighten up your last moments in government servitude. Nice classical allusion, though. If there's anything I can do to ease the pain – "

"There's something you can tell me, Eejit." Wishart's voice was imperfectly even. "But you'll have to bear in mind that I'm still a serving customs officer. If only just."

The Trojan acknowledged Wishart's waning temporal authority with the faintest possible elevation of one eyebrow.

"Excuse me, Mr. Eejit," put in Alvin Cricker, who was beginning to feel neglected. "I'd like to remind you that the Earth Federation has granted a general amnesty for all, ahem, crimes committed against it by Beltides during the Unfriendly Years."

"I do believe you're right, Mr. . . . Alvin Cricker, isn't it? Worlds-famous author of *The Marsport Nobody Knows.* Stuff like that. And I really must point out that the Earth Federation is in no ethical position to issue amnesties – for anything. Least of all to law-abiding Beltides such as myself.

"Point taken – a very sore point."

Meanwhile, Wishart was thinking resentfully of the gentle way Old Father Time had dealt with his honourable opponent. Buck Eejit must have been at least fifty standard years old, but his tawny mane was disconcertingly grey-hair free. Nor did there seem to be much superfluous fat on his burly frame. He considered his own wide-parted white hair and the abdominal spread that had started long before the onset of middle age.

"Trojan." Wishart spoke with exaggerated calm. "Just what *were* you smuggling into the Asteroid Belt, over all those years?"

"There's no reason why I shouldn't tell you, Dunky, the grand way things have turned out. Especially for me." But Buck Eejit held his verbal fire until: "Spaceships!"

THE ILLUSTRATED BOY

1

"I'm Illustrated, Doctor Langford."

The four-fifth naked boy on my couch smiled up at me, impishly.

"I can see that, all right. But . . . *why*?"

"You've heard of 'The Illustrated Man'?"

"Yes . . ."

"Well, I'm his son – Brad."

I couldn't think of a suitable reply, not that the boy waited for one.

"Of course, I have fewer Illustrations than Dad, and the stories they tell are much shorter. Mini-sagas, really."

"'Mini-sagas' – "

"Fifty words long, exactly, not counting the titles. Vignettes, if you prefer."

"Can you show me a few samples, Brad?"

"Watch."

2

The first Illustration flickered into life, along with its telepathic mini-saga.
ONE: 'BANSHEE'.

A banshee howled.

"The banshee's cry means death."

Ballard, an American prospector, had been so informed by his ex-partner, Egan, whom he'd just strangled. They had discovered gold in the Sperrin mountains.

"Appropriate," Ballard mused. Then he stumbled over a cliff-edge to his death.

The banshee howls *before* someone dies.

Brad, the Illustrated Boy, shifted restlessly on the couch, and – each time he shifted – another Illustration came into view, highlighting his arms, his chest, his belly-button.

TWO: 'THE KILKENNY CATAPULT'.

"Red alert! Atomic attack!"

Doctor James Kilkenny never actually heard the end of that announcement. But then, neither did anybody else at Blare Hospital.

The blast of the first super-duper neutron bomb hurled him through time to the relative safety of the twenty-fourth century . . .where he died of radiation sickness.

The Illustrated Boy shifted again.

THREE: 'LOOP'.

"There is no such thing as a time reversor."

Doctor Qui was speaking to his young son, Sandy."

"That's what *you* think, Dad" said the boy.

Sandy pointed a strange device at his father, who merely laughed and turned away, repeating:

".reversor time a as thing such no is There"

And again.

FOUR: 'THE INIMITABLE DICKENS'.

Martin Lydecker was a writer, or – rather – a Literary Technician.

He glared at the display screen of HACK (Hi-Tech Artistic Computer Kit).

"Someday I'll be a *real* writer – just like Honey Wells."

Lydecker took an antique ball-point pen and scribbled the first sentence of his original masterpiece:

I am born.

and . . .

FIVE:'TOUCH NOT THE CAT'.

Ed Katzenjammer had hated cats ever since his first day at school.

En route to work one morning, Ed's path was crossed by a black tomcat. He kicked it – hard.

That night, another cat *miaow*-ed near him. He kicked out . . . and an escaped black panther tore off his right leg.

The Illustrated Boy shifted yet again. This time, however, only one word-image appeared: PAUSE.

3

It was all over, within five minutes and/or 250 words.

I had seen all the Illustrations. Or, rather, all of them that Brad *wanted* me to see.

He was sleeping. I checked his pulse. It was regular, untroubled.

There was, it seemed, only one clear space remaining upon the Illustrated Boy's exposed body; his right big toe.

And, even as I watched, a face formed itself on the nail. *My* face.

Another mini-saga in the making?

More images took definite shape, until the complete picture showed the Illustrated Boy holding a large water-pistol. It was aimed straight at my face.

I ran out of the consulting room. Fast. I didn't want to see this particular mini-saga work itself out.

Don't look back –

"Doctor Langford."

SPLASH!

"Hi, Doc. I'm Brad's twin brother – Doug."

SEA CHANGES

Derek Crown, perennial student and would-be *bon vivant*, was being held captive by a mad scientist.

The truth, if it must be told, lay in the mean between two extremes. His name was Derek Crown, and he had been an undergraduate at New England's venerable Peskatonic University for more years than any normal person remembers without shame. He dreamed of living the good life, *à la* Maupassant's Bel Ami, but he lacked a social *je ne sais quoi.* Also money, and the ability to earn same.

Fortunately, his white-haired and well-off widowed mother back home in Redknob, Nebraska, sent him a regular – if, he felt, piffling – monthly allowance.

And Derek was being held captive, after a fashion, in his own Arkwich City collegiate rooms. His quasi-captor was Professor Ichabod Avenel, who may not have been a mad scientist, but he certainty didn't fit most people's definition of sane.

The professor looked demented. There was no other just word to describe him. Colleagues said, perhaps unkindly, that he lived in hopes of one day winning a Nobel Prize for chemistry. Or physics. Or mathematics. Or . . . anything, really.

But Derek Crown, himself, could not have been called an oil painting, or even a water colour. He was tall but bent over, with carroty red hair now beating a rapid retreat. In academic matters, Derek was clever enough for most purposes. But, as countless teachers had so succinctly put it, he was lazy-minded.

Spring sunshine streamed in through the grimy, ill-made windows. It illuminated the grimy, ill-made living room with its grimy, ill-made furniture. Background music was provided by *Head* a 1968 film starring the Monkees, Frank Zappa, and Victor Mature. But the ancient TV speakers made for a tinny effect. It made Derek feel nostalgic for his half-semester at some film school in California. Or was it Nevada . . . ?

Professor Avenel sat poised like a humanoid helix on the edge of a rickety cane chair. His normally saturnine face was flushed and animated. There was a gleam in his misty grey eyes. "Science says you're wrong if you believe that reality is a physical constant. It's just a matter of collective opinion."

"Yawn."

But Professor Avenel was unperturbed by Derek's patented enthusiastic apathy. He went on and on: "Diluted presentation . . . vibratory planes . . . perception thresholds . . . classic paper entitled 'The Endochronic Properties of Resublimated . . .'"

Derek continued browsing through the tome on his lap: (Isaac) *Asimov's Guide to Shakespeare.* (William) Shakespeare, that is.

"I'm supposed to be majoring in English Literature, not science," he sub-vocalized. "Jane Austen, Charles Dickens, Harlan Ellison – stuff like that. I only took that bloody awful psychophysics course because it sounded like something out of a science-fiction novel."

". . . Thiotimoline'."

"Tim O'Theolean?" Derek glanced abstractedly up from the chapter dissecting *Troilus and Cressida.* "That name rings a bell."

"Thio-*tim*-oline. It's a chemical substance, not some Irish proper name."

A blank stare was the professor's only reward.

"Thiotimoline is one of the more *outré* hallucinogenic agents," he snapped. "My in-depth researches have led me to believe that, properly formulated, it can condition the human mind into perceiving alternative planes of reality."

"Something like an LSD trip?"

"*Nothing* like an LSD trip."

"Have it your own way, Prof."

'Prof' Avenel took Derek at his sardonic word. "Thiotimoline is, simply speaking, a psychological catalyst. It stimulates the brain into a much higher mode of time/space perception. According to my experiments, at any rate."

The word 'experiments' touched off a RED ALERT signal in Derek's mind. He said, anxiously: "And now you're looking for a guinea pig – a human guinea pig."

"Yes."

"And you'd like me to . . ."

"Volunteer. That's right."

Derek was about to Brando-speak "Find yourself another boy." Then a mercenary instinct gave him pause. Instead, he asked: "What's in it for me?"

"A passing grade in psychophysics."

"Big deal. The answer is no. N-O. No!"

"*Mister* Crown, I must ask you to reconsider." Derek could hear the disparaging italics in the old boy's voice. "Not to put too fine a point on it, you – *sir* – are a piss artist."

"Now look he- "

"No – *you* look *here*. Dean Swallow told you just the other day that he is dead set on having you from dismissed from Peskatonic University at the end of this semester. Unless your work, for the want of a better

113

word, shows a dramatic improvement in the meantime."

"Blackmail!"

"Right you are."

Derek took mental stock of his situation.

I couldn't get to first base in a psychophysics exam. And he must know from Dr. Donny Ghoulart that I'm barely scraping through Eng. Lit. If I'm slung out of yet another university, Mother has threatened to cut off my allowance – PDQ.

Aloud, he sycophanted: "Please excuse my little joke – sir. I'd be glad to help you push back the frontiers of science."

"Congratulations – Derek. As they say, one volunteer is worth ten pressed men." The professor permitted his lips to loosen in the semblance of a smile. "Don't worry. I'll square things for you with the doomy-gloomy Dean."

"I'm ready when you are, Ichabod. I mean, sir." Derek dredged up a smidgin of his schoolboy French. "*Allons-y!*"

"There is no reason for us to *aller* anywhere. This room will do nicely, for my – our – purposes."

"Really?" Derek looked about him. "I wouldn't have thought . . ."

"Familiar surroundings should provide us with useful ontological contrasts. And I've got all the necessary equipment, here, in this gadget bag."

Professor Avenel placed the aforesaid receptacle on the living-room table, raising a not inconsiderable cloud of dust in the process. Then he happily set about removing vials, hypodermic syringes, meters, and other scientific bric-à-brac.

Meanwhile, Derek's overweening natural cowardice was reasserting itself. "Is there a watchamacallit – antidote for this thiotimoline stuff?"

"Of course there is an antidote. It's ready and waiting, just in case things go wrong."

"What?"

"Which they won't. Probably."

"Then we might as well get this medicine show on the road. 'Lay on, Macduff – '"

"Hold, enough!"

In less time that it takes a hypothetical observer to tell, the experiment was completed.

"But I don't understand." Scientific detachment had fed Professor Avenel's mental coop. He was, in fact, jumping up and down. "It *ought* to have worked."

"Take it easy, sir." Derek Crown was the very model of solicitude. "You can't win them all, as that banker in Monte Carlo once said. Back to old drawing board, *n'est-ce pas?*"

Professor Avenel followed Derek's Gallic lead. "*Oui, mon brave. Vous avez raison.*"

"That's *le billet* – I mean, that's the ticket."

"I've overlooked something, somewhere, somehow. Psychophysics may not be an exact science, after all. The devil is in the details. I can't see the wood for the trees. Check, re-check . . "

". . . and check again. The good old scientific method. But I'm sure you'll solve the problem. Whatever it might turn out to be. Thiotimoline will yield up its secrets, sooner or later."

"Thank you, Derek, for those few kind words." The crestfallen scientist managed a slight accession of cheerfulness, and even some atypical concern. "You don't seem to be suffering from any ill-effects. But I'd recommend a thorough medical examination. Today, if possible."

Derek was feeling a bit light-headed, but – at the same time – more healthy than he had ever been in his life. However, the living room did look a bit fuzzy and the professor's voice seemed to be reaching him from a vasty distance. His own spoken words held an echoing quality:

"You're welcome, sir. And don't worry about me. I'll phone Doc Norseman first thing in the morning, even before my regular jog around Peripheral Park. I'm only sorry that I couldn't have been of more help to you."

"Never you mind, young man." Professor Avenel looked a bit puzzled, but also strangely content. "You kept your side of the bargain. Rest assured that I'll keep mine."

"Uh – "

"The passing grade in psychophysics will be forthcoming, and you may forget all about Dean Swallow's expulsion threat."

Derek had missed most, if not all, of the professor's little speech. He felt a sudden need to inventory the microcosm about him. The living room had taken on a darkling aspect, although the rich furnishings lent it a splendid dash of colour. There was also a warm glow from the genuine coal fire – Derek's atavistic pride and joy.

Then Derek turned his attention to the wintry world beyond the frost-patterned picture window. The snowstorm had abated significantly, but a mini-blizzard still huffed and puffed along the almost deserted street. Evening was, by now, quite well advanced.

Artificial daylight bathed the living room as Derek hand-flicked on the nearest proximity switch. The illumination was tasteful, but adequate, with no unseemly glare. He gazed in quiet satisfaction around his neat little hearth and home.

Professor Avenel had just finished packing up his gadget bag when the lights came on. He blinked – more in surprise than anything else – then said, ruefully: "Well, I'd better be getting along. Good afternoon, Derek. And thanks again, for all your help."

"Good evening, sir. And *I* should jolly well be thanking *you*." He stole a glance at the professor's slight form. "Wrap yourself up cosily, now. It must be freezing out there."

"'Evening'?"

"I'll see you early tomorrow morning. Just before I go to the Dean's office." Derek smiled in joyful anticipation. "We can brainstorm the last few chapters of my doctoral thesis on psychophysics. There are still some rough edges to be smoothed out."

"'Doctoral thesis'?"

"That's right, Professor Avenel." Derek spoke in hurt surprise. "The one I've been working on for nearly two years."

"'Two years'?" The professor gave him a vague glance and an even vaguer smile. There was a question-mark expression on his face. Moments later, Derek watched him shuffle off into the sombre night and the fluttering snow.

The tides of time rolled on.

Professor Ichabod Avenel squinted his eyes against the slanting rays of the mid-afternoon sun. It was a longish walk back to his rooms in Porlock Hall, and the humid air caused him some discomfort. He had, however, much more pressing things than the weather on his mind.

"Thiotimoline really does work, even if there is a delayed action effect with human beings. Derek Crown is now living in a world of his own. A world which represents the exact opposite of his normal physical and mental environment. I'd better restore him to his real self, pretty damned quick. The impli- "

He chuckled, rustily, then went on:

"'You can't win them all' – hah! The antidote will bring him back to common space/time, sure enough. But perhaps residual traces of thiotimoline will turn the old, worthless Derek Crown into a new, worthwhile human being."

The professor's humanitarian concern for the redemption of his dwarf-star pupil lasted for fifteen whole seconds. After a thoughtful silence, he resumed talking to himself like some other person altogether. An Edwardian actor-manager, mayhap, or Richard Dawkins on speed.

"My fellow Nobel laureates, ladies and gentlemen, members of the international Press corps. Please try to keep up with me. I have proved that the perception of change poses a very real psychophysical problem. What *is* ceases to be and is transformed into something rich and strange. Perceptions are not static. We must distinguish between continuous change and . . ."

Meanwhile, the subjectively born-again Derek Crown had returned to the cozy environs of his living room. "Home sweet home. Away from home." He looked with keen interest at the film version of Raymond Chandler's last novel, *Rewind*, which was flickering across the wide-format TV screen.

"Robert Mitchum was just the right age to play Philip Marlowe, in 1958. What if they'd cast him in the part fifteen years later. Why, it doesn't bear thinking about."

Then he headed for his antique roll-top desk.

"I'd better add the finishing touches to that monograph on psycho-biological time paradoxes for *Ion* magazine." The very light of science shone in his eyes. "Publish or be damned – as dear old Dean Swallow might misquote it. In any case, I've already sent the advance money to Mother."

Abrupt mental side-turn. "But I've still got time for a little light reading. All work and no play . . ." Derek sat down in his plush easy chair, before the suitably roaring fire. Then he took up the thick volume which he'd been perusing before Professor Avenel's unexpected arrival:

Shakespeare's Guide to Asimov.

FLY FORGOTTEN, AS A DREAM

Ferguson here – John Ferguson.

I'm a free-lance journalist, and – more to the point – an acknowledged expert on such pseudo-sciences as spiritualism and parapsychology. A confirmed sceptic who has debunked many a crackpot theory in my best-selling book, *The Supernatural – Who Needs It?* More than six months on the *New York Times* list, with a sequel well in the works.

Or at least I used to be a confirmed sceptic, until Diana Weaver came along. She was Diana Summers when I'd first met her, during our university days. We've been close friends ever since – though not close enough, for my liking. She became an advertising copywriter, while I . . . But I've already told you too much about me.

For Diana (she hated 'Di') Weaver, it all began about six weeks after her husband, Paul, had been killed in a freak car accident. Diana had been driving the car, and Paul's death had hit her hard.

I'm a just-the-facts-ma'am journalist type, not an airy-fairy fiction writer. Some unkind people, editors among them, might disagree with me there. I felt, however, that the deep background to this particular story could best be presented through a process of dramatic reconstruction. I've had to put many unverifiable thoughts into Diana's head and ditto words in her mouth. But I'm sure she won't – or wouldn't – hold that against me.

At the same time, I must be as honest as humanly possible about Whatever Happened to the Weavers. No glossing over the difficult bits with a veneer of would-be deathless prose. I read Bob Shaw's invaluable *How to Write Science Fiction* (Allison & Busby, London, 1993: look out for it!) before starting work. The following passage *re* 'deathless prose' has been postited – is there really such an ugly word? – to my computer terminal:

> That was self-deception of the worst kind, even had I had enough literary skill to pull off the trick. Firstly, because a writer should *always* be doing his best – otherwise he is wasting his time and talent; secondly, the reader is not so easily fooled.

Words of wisdom, Mr. Shaw.

One more thing. I don't regret not being able or willing to discuss personkind's essential nature in terms that would please admirers of so-called naturalistic fiction. John O'Hara. Thomas and Tom Wolfe. Frank McCourt. Anybody who maintains, against contrary evidence that THE TRUTH IS ALWAYS SIMPLE. As I've said before (in *The Supernatural – Who Needs It?*): "The shibboleth of 'simple truth' has kept too many otherwise clever people simple-minded for millennia."

Deathless prose or what? Which reminds me. I also had to avoid one of my more grievous faults – flippancy. "The name is Doctor Axe, psychic detective, and this is my most recent case." No, that would never do.

"Diana Weaver came home from work – just as usual – and her throat tightened – again, just as usual – as she turned the corner into Bloomfield Close. She still found it unbearable to realize that Paul would not be waiting for her." Yes, that's the idea . . .

"It's the little things we miss after a close relationship has ended. That old Joni Mitchell song was right. You really don't know what you've got till it's gone." After a long pause: "I wonder if sleep will come

121

to me tonight. And, if it does, whether I'll dream of Paul. Again."

Diana stood in the middle of the street, gazing wistfully at the ordinary-looking house which had once seemed so extraordinary. Then something out of joint caught her eye. The front gate, which ran the full width of the driveway, was open, at a forty-five degree angle.

"That's funny. I could have sworn – "

Still puzzled, but with many more pressing matters on her mind, Diana made to enter the driveway. Then she walked up against the suddenly re-closed gate.

"Let me see, now. The gate *looks* all right." She tapped one of the gate-panels, twice. "It *feels* perfectly normal. And there isn't even the suspicion of a breeze. No – I've just got to pull myself together."

Diana opened the gate and stepped inside. Then she latched it shut, with exaggerated care.

There was no logical explanation as to why 'it' happened, or began to happen, that night instead of any other night. Diana was convinced that the gate had been open. But she also had the equally strong conviction that it had, in fact, been closed.

"*Déjà vu*," she told herself, trying to make an old, bad joke out of it. "All over again."

Thankfully, Diana slept soundly that night – and without dreaming. When she awoke, at six-thirty on the dot, her muscles were tense and knotted. This marked the beginning of what had developed into a daily ritual.

Diana always had to bear in mind that Paul wasn't there beside her. If she forgot and turned to embrace him, finding empty sheets, the agony of being alive when he was dead proved intolerable. Today, however, she had the Front Gate Mystery to ponder.

"The facts are clear enough. I actually saw the gate lying open, and there's no such thing as mirages here in Bloomfield Close. It felt solid to the touch – *very* solid. In rational terms, as John Ferguson would say, it can only have been some kind of delusion. But my memory insists that it *did* happen that way."

Deep in thought (*There might be a way of making sure*), Diana walked to the downtown Vee Packard advertising agency where she worked as a senior copywriter. After the accident, she'd suffered from a morbid fear of driving; even public transport or taxis made her nervous. And the office was, after all, only twenty minutes away by foot.

Ever since Paul's violent death, she'd formed a love/hate relationship with her job. Credit side: editorial work required much coherent, if not always constructive, thought. Depression could temporarily be held at bay. Debit side: something usually happened that would have amused Paul. It was particularly painful when tactless colleagues swapped anecdotes about their own still-intact families.

When Diana walked home that late afternoon, she carried a loaded Polaroid camera that had been left in the stock room after some long-forgotten office party. "This should help me to clear things up." Talking to herself enabled her to cope with being lonely rather than just alone.

The cosy little close had a secluded air about it, and – of course – there was no through traffic. Weather conditions were milder than usual for early September, with a cloudless sky redly suffused by the setting sun.

"Camera's ready. The front gate seems to be firmly closed. Still ... I'd better do a dry run." Diana took a deep breath, then opened the gate. But her very first stride was cut short as she walked straight into the gate.

"I'd *opened* the gate. There was nothing for me to run up against – nothing at all! Yet my knee hurts where it hit the closed gate that should have been wide open. There's no sense to it."

She stood stock-still for an uncounted while. Then a gust of wind blew the cobwebs from her mind.

"Nothing ventured, nothing gained." Diana stepped back to the middle of the street, aimed the camera, then pressed the shutter. The glare from the inbuilt flash dazzled her a bit, but – when she put out her hand – the gate was open.

Diana entered the house, almost forgetting to close the front door behind her. She hung up her coat, walked into the living room, and sat down in an easy chair.

The developed print was very distinct, at least in its peripheral details. It resembled a still from some special-effects movie, showing the front of her house in the background and . . . something else up front. "Inkblot test." She might have been looking at her front gate – once open and once closed – in the self-same photograph. Or it might have been an amorphous mess caused by chemically-imbalanced film that should have been used months, if not years, before.

"Double, triple, *multiple* exposure?" Diana let go of the photograph; it fluttered to the floor. "In any case, it proves sweet-damn-all." Then, mingling tiredness with bad temper: "I need a different kind of proof!"

Diana went to the cocktail cabinet, reached for an unopened bottle of Moskovskaya vodka. "Thank you, Big John Ferguson. That book-signing jaunt round the former Soviet Union wasn't entirely wasted, after all." Then another bottle, on the nearby occasional table, gave her pause. It was either half-full or half-empty, depending upon one's karmic viewpoint.

"Maker's Mark Kentucky straight bourbon – specially imported." Diana shook her head. "But that was Paul's favourite before- and after-dinner drink. I converted the last bottle into a candle-holder weeks ago. That red-wax effect on the neck . . ." She checked out the mantelpiece, over against the opposite wall. "Yes, it's still there."

Beside the Maker's Mark was a miniature bottle of Ballygowan spring water – not specially imported.

"Paul's favourite mixer." Diana touched both bottles, half-hoping for an illusion-breaking *pop!*, but they were real enough. As was the tumbler beside them, which she hadn't noticed before. Sudden anger made her rattle the glassware with a downward slap. "Mrs. Lunn!"

Diana's overwrought imagination went into an even higher gear. Perhaps there had been one remaining bottle of Maker's Mark, and the cleaning woman she employed had helped herself to a free drink. "No, that horse won't run." The still, small voice of reason told her that Mrs. Lunn had completed her once-weekly stint the day before yesterday – and that she was a dour Calvanistic teetotaler.

"One . . . two . . . three" Diana looked away from the table and kept on counting up to ten. Then fifteen, for good measure. After which time the bottle of bourbon was still there, but the tumbler and spring-water miniature had somehow been cleared away.

"Am I going mad?" It was an unanswerable question. Instead, Diana tried to reason out the weird phenomena. But, as always, they added up to mere hallucinations. She crossed the living room and stood pensively over Paul's rather chunky writing desk.

"I'll set the whole thing down on paper." She spoke softly, as if weighing each word for a hidden meaning. "Check and re-check every last detail. The good old scientific method." Then, much faster: "What's that on the desk-top?"

Diana passed a hand across her forehead. "Why, it's Paul's five year diary; the one I bought for him, last Christmas. Five whole years. Paul didn't even make it through one of them."

Shocked by this abrupt encounter with her all-too-recent past, Diana struggled to maintain a foothold in the present. But the present was a cold mockery without Paul. The past seemed to be a much more alluring place. Images of Paul flashed before her mind's eye, images that were cinematically exact. Colour, Panavision, full stereoscopic sound. She would never be in the market for a VR helmet.

Diana's painfully eidetic memory flashed back to the first time she had formally met Paul Weaver, nine years before. She'd been eighteen-year-old Diana Summers, back then, just about to start her freshperson year at King's University. It was a flat-warming party, given by somebody she didn't really know at the time and couldn't remember now. Real spur-of-the-moment stuff.

John Ferguson had made a big thing out of driving her to the party in his father's birthday-cum-graduation present. "A bright yellow Lotus Esprit," she recalled aloud. "Perhaps just that little bit *too* bright. Like John himself, I suppose – bright, not yellow."

But the dominant-male Ferguson redeemed himself in Diana's eyes by bringing her into social contact with Paul Weaver, who had never really shone at such large-scale social gatherings. Like Diana, Paul was an arts student. And, as it later turned out, he took an obsessive interest in all printed matter that came his way. Sauce-bottle labels were treated, by him, as if they were miniature Rosetta Stones.

"Bookworm," was the key word in 'Big' John Ferguson's I-even-talk-to-losers character assassination speech.

Ferguson had, in fact, been digging his conversational grave with his own mouth; not for the first time, nor the last. He never did learn when not to stop talking, let alone heed negative inter-personal vibes. The same thing could fairly be said about his writing style, as even the bitchiest book reviewers became tired of pointing out.

By stark contrast, the neither tall nor short Paul Weaver had a build that the word 'slight' described to a T. Diana felt like a redheaded Xena – Warrior Princess standing beside him. But there was an indefinable something in the way his hazel eyes glinted in the half-light of the room.

"I don't count that as an introduction," he said to Diana, looking her straight in the eye. A shy smile disarmed any possible accusation of sarcasm. "My name is Paul Weaver, and I'm very pleased to meet *you*. Diana, isn't it?"

"That's right . . . Paul."

John Ferguson had been verbally overpowered, reeling back and left for dead near the kitchenette refrigerator. He seemed to take it well enough, however, remaining close friends with Paul and – especially – Diana.

Once in a great while, (paraphrasing Diana's first and permanent impression) someone like Paul Weaver reminds us that being polite is not a sign of weakness and that nice people don't always finish last. Paul might have been thoughtless, at times, but he never meant ill. He was also something of a drifter, just about falling into his job as Human Resources Director with the 'Barrowby Boys' media empire. People trusted him on sight, and he made it a point of honour not to let any halfway decent person down.

They were married within four years of that official first meeting. John Ferguson acted as Paul's best man at the wedding; 'acted' being very much the operative word. The marriage seemed to have been Made in Heaven, as those they-people so tweely put it. But Fate had other, more complex plans for Paul and Diana Weaver.

"Some day I might read his diary," Diana said at last. "But not now . . . not now." Then, with sudden realization: "Why is it lying about here in plain sight? Paul always locked it away in a desk-drawer."

Diana opened the diary, flinched as she saw Paul's near-microscopic handwriting. Then something else came to her notice. "Strange. There's a pen thrust between the pages like a place-marker." She riffled through the pages. "The writing is Paul's, all right, and the date on the page is . . . today's date."

The diary fell on to the desk-top. Diana stood rigid; every muscle taut, every nerve strained to the breaking point.

It was at least two minutes before Diana could bring herself to re-open the diary. By that time, she had arrived at what seemed to be a perfectly logical explanation. "Maybe Paul hadn't restricted himself to the assigned spaces when he had something extra to say, but kept writing past the correct date." Yes – that was it.

Even so, Diana had to stave off the indelicate moment with delaying tactics. "Leathersmith of London." She turned the diary over and over in her

hands. "5" x 8" – or should that be 10cm. x 16cm.?"
Then she finally read the most recent page. The letters
were a little more askew than usual, for Paul, but still
quite legible:

> It's been six weeks since the accident. Things don't
> seem to be any easier. If anything, they're getting much
> worse. I keep waiting at the front gate for Diana to come
> home from work. She usually got here just after me. Or was
> it the other way round? My memory is on the blink again.

Diana retreated behind an aegis of non-
thinking/non-being for what seemed like hours, but
which was actually just a few moments. When she
came back to herself, the diary was gone, and there was
no pen between her fingers. But she distinctly
remembered scrawling a message underneath Paul's
last – or was it latest? – entry:

> Paul – in God's name, where are you? This is Diana.
> I'm not dead. I thought you were. Please answer me –
> where are you?

"It's impossible!" Diana could almost feel the
exclamation mark in her mind. She fought her way
back to near-normality. "Nothing like . . . that . . .
really happened. It must have been another delusion,
like the front gate with an intermittent life of its own."

Diana spent a restless, pillow-tossed night. She'd
always prided herself on placing no credence in the
supernatural otherworld. "Ghoulies and ghosties and
long-legged beasties" or things that go bump in the
night had never made her tremble. Now, however, she
wasn't quite so sure.

But the evidence, despite being a shade
insubstantial, was still there. If only in mental form.
Nor did any palpable menace surround the
'reappearance' of her dead husband. Those words
'dead' and 'husband' still kept their power to hurt her,

no matter how many weeks had passed since the accident.

Diana telephoned the office, in succinct sentences: "Hello . . . Sidney?"/"It's me, Diana."/"No, I'm calling in sick."/"Some kind of bug."/"Thank you – a friend is need is a friend indeed." "Be seeing you soonest."/*Click!*

What Diana told Sidney McDonald had been the unvarnished truth. She was suffering from a lack of sleep that exacerbated her already weakened mental and physical condition. Also, she needed *time* – time in which to think and plan her next move.

After an indulgent breakfast of bacon, fried eggs, and pork sausages, Diana sat down in her favourite easy chair. She'd made herself a second cup of Blue Mountain coffee. As she set the cup down on the occasional table, it clinked against a tumbler which had gone unnoticed before. The contents, at least, were familiar.

"Paul always had a before-breakfast drink of Omnivit – or whatever they call that New Age concoction." It had been a running gag between them. But Diana didn't feel much like laughing, under the circumstances. Especially when the tumbler disappeared between blinks. "I'd better check up on something else . . ."

Paul's diary had been returned to his writing desk, with a brass paperweight laid across its open pages. Diana could see yesterday's entry, if such a thing were possible, plus her own hectic message. And beyond that:

> Diana, darling, I believe you wrote to me as if you're still alive. Maybe I'm crazy to answer you like this. But if you really *are* alive – somewhere, somehow.

Diana picked up the 'vintage' Polaroid camera. The shutter clicked, the flash-bulb hissed like a hot poker thrust into cold mead. When the mini-nova had run its course, Paul's diary was again nowhere to be seen.

"One elephant, two elephant, three . . ."

The eventual dried-out print showed the open pages quite clearly. However, the words Diana knew to be written there could no longer be read; by the naked eye, at any rate. "But I can't ignore the evidence of my own senses." She sort-of smiled. "Or is that just famous last words?"

Diana felt another of her recent near-panic urges coming on. Leave the house. Go somewhere – anywhere – that wasn't here. Flight, not fight, seemed like the best survivalist imperative. This time, however, she willed herself into writing a thngs-to-be-done list. Paul had often joked that a Master List of her all-time lists would reach from Earth to Pluto and back again – twice.

"There's many a true word . . ."

It was only a two-item shopping list, but Diana thought long and hard before putting her pen to paper. "Examination technique. Take time, make time. *Think* about the question. List all salient points. Start answer when ready." Scribble, scribble, scribble. Then, satisfied with the result, she quickly encarred (for the first time in three weeks) and drove mallwards.

"I'm a shopper, but Paul was a buyer." Diana didn't let the light mid-morning traffic flow interrupt her exterior monologue. "No browsing or second-and-more thoughts for him. He always knew exactly what he wanted to buy and bought it. As for Post Office queues . . . talk about the Incredible Sulk."

She tried not to laugh at her own little joke, with some degree of failure.

A Paul-like swoop of Vixon's discount store resulted in the purchase of a Minolta Dimãge 5 SLR-type camera fitted with a 35-250m F/2.8-3.5 non-interchangeable GT lens.

"Part of our Dimãge Limitation Exercize" quipped the male salesperson, making Diana wish that she *had* laughed more at her own little joke. She also endured quickfire info-dumping about maximum image sizes ("2048 x 1536 pixels from its 3.3-millions-pixel sensor") and PC files ("Images may be recorded in one of four sizes with any of five compression modes").

Diana bought some more magic-box stuff, which made the salesperson's grin wax seemingly wider than his already flat-iron face. Then she went home and did whatever the manuals told her could be done with the equipment plus anything else that came to her mind. After which . . .

"I'm dazzled by all this hi-tech wizardry. Boys and their toys, indeed. But there's one way of putting it to the acid test. I'll consult the biggest boy I know – John Ferguson. Yes, *he'll* know how to sort things out."

"John," said Diana Weaver, after she had settled herself down in Ferguson's bachelor apartment. "I want you to look at a set of photographs and tell me if you see what I see – or don't see."

"Is this some kind of – "

"Believe me, this is no joke. I may be mad, but I'm no practical joker."

"Right you are, Diana. I'll try to keep an open mind."

Diana passed a manila file-folder across the skeletal coffee table to Ferguson, who took his own sweet time about half-opening it. She bore in mind that

John was never at a loss for words when there was nothing much to be said; only important matters gave him any conversational pause. He might have been thinking . . .

And, Diana told herself, I know just what he's thinking *about*. John Ferguson must have been an exclusively bottle-fed baby. The eyes had it, all right, falling just short of X-ray vision. She tried not to draw any deep, distracting breaths.

"A-*hem*."

"Sorry, Diana." Ferguson almost ripped the file-folder fully open. "I was just . . ."

"Thinking."

"That's right. Ha-ha. And now I'll start looking – at the photos." A nervously louder *ha-ha*.

Ferguson suited the actions to his words, beginning with the front-gate Polaroid snapshot. He subjected it to a close scrutiny, using the naked eye followed by a rather Holmesian magnifying glass. To Diana, it still looked like a crazy picture of two doors, nearly at right angles – in the same gate-frame and hung from the same hinges.

"Two gates in the same gate-frame. At the very same time," Ferguson said, echoing her unspoken thoughts. Then he took a line of attack: "Diana, I never knew that you were keen on trick photography."

"'Trick photography'?"

"It's a competent job." Ferguson ignored Diana's evident bristling. "You simply covered half the film and exposed with the portal closed, then exposed for the other half with the portal open. Well matched, though. You must have used a tripod."

"No tripod, John. Or even a portal – whatever *that* might be. Correct me if I'm wrong – and you always do – but aren't Polaroid cameras somewhat limited when it comes to trick photography?"

"Well, if you'd used one of the old-style Polaroids, where the film remains in the camera until it's pulled down . . ."

Ferguson adopted what Diana called his if-you-listen-to-me-you-might-learn-something persona. He told her that Dr. Edwin H. Land had marketed his first 'instant camera' in 1948. Coloured dyes passed from a negative on to a film inside a sealed unit, producing a print after sixty-odd seconds. The process . . . blah-blah-blah.

"Look at the next photograph, John."

Ferguson took a much-needed break for breath. He eyed the second Polaroid print with the air of an indulgent adult humouring a bright, if fanciful, child. Then his attitude became more serious. "Writing . . . can't make it out." Using the magnifying glass, he read what was photographed on the pages of a diary that hadn't – apparently – been before the camera.

"It *looks* like Paul's handwriting, sure enough." Ferguson handed the file-folder back to Diana. "Have you taken any other photos – with a real camera?"

"Yes, with a real – and digital – camera. But I haven't transferred the memory card to my PC, for editing."

"Or you could use the new Image Matching Technology, developed by – "

"Have you got an explanation, John?" Diana cut in. "I can't think of one. That is, one that makes any kind of sense."

Ferguson looked more than a little miffed. "Give me some more . . . background material."

"Playing for time, eh?" Diana actually showed signs of good humour. "I can give you the *what* and the *when*, but not the *how* or the *why*."

Diana went on to tell Ferguson everything that had happened so far, with no attempts at psychobabble or self-justification. At first he simply stared at her, then his reporter's instinct for a good story was caught and held. When she had finished her account:

"That's a ripping yarn, Diana. I take it that you've eliminated the supernatural?"

"Yes, of course."

"Good girl. Now, let me put a case to *you*."

"Fire away . . . boy."

"Once, back when I was a humble courts reporter" – Diana looked askance at that one – "I covered a case in which a woman accused a man of raping her. She was totally sincere in this belief. But her own family testified that she'd made the marks on herself. To cap it all, there was no medical evidence supporting her accusation."

"You're suggesting, therefore, that I might have faked all that evidence in order to comfort myself – ten forgotten about the act of faking?"

"I'm not suggesting anything. Yet." Faraway look. "The time to make up your mind about people is never! That's from *The Philadelphia* – "

" – *Story*." Diana cast her face against any off-the-wall movie memorabilia. "Frankly, John, I'm insulted by your implicit accusation of fakery on my part. And we can forget about this milk-of-amnesia theory."

"I didn't mean . . ."

"So what's left."

Ferguson, a long way short of gruntled, spent a bitter time-out before taking another shot at Diana's problem. He mumbled something about "marshalling his thoughts." Then, trying to sound authoritative:

"This snap of the front gate still looks like an incredibly perfect piece of trick photography. I can't see the place where the two exposures join, even under high magnification. Some people – experts not excluded – might be taken in by it. But . . . "

"That doesn't get you very far. You're back-pedalling, in fact."

"As you say." Ferguson gave her a Patrick McGoohan under-the-eyebrows glare. "Then let's consider the road accident in which Paul was . . . killed."

Diana didn't so much as blink back at him.

"The two of you were driving home, behind an overloaded truck hauling soil, uprooted branches, concrete blocks – general garden garbage. Paul was at the wheel. A child ran in front of the truck. Its driver slammed on the brakes. But your car slid on the wet road surface before . . . Do you really want me to continue, Diana?"

"Yes, John. I'll be all right."

"You almost rammed the back of the truck, the tailgate of which gave way. A heavy marble bench smashed through the windshield. It could have hit you, Diana. Or it could have missed both of you. By sheer chance, it happened to hit Paul."

"But it could just as easily have been me." Diana's voice hit a higher emotional level. "And that diary entry is written as if it *had* been me. Don't you see, John?"

The answer came back as "*Harumph*."

Time didn't so much stand still as cease to exist for an indeterminate while. It was a study in polar opposites. Diana Weaver fair, slim, intense; John

Ferguson dour, hefty, withdrawn. The silence of stone, personified.

Ferguson blinked first. "I really do think you've acted just like the girl in that court case." Then he adopted what was, for him, a more sympathetic attitude. "No offense, Diana, but have you seen a doctor? About, you know . . ."

"None taken, John." Diana managed an adequate smile. "I haven't seen a doctor. Not even a trick cyclist what you'd call a trick cyclist. Not yet. Sometime, soon. "She leant forward in her chair. "But please try to rationalize my delusions first. If you possibly can."

Ferguson leant back in his chair. "What I'm about to propose would be rejected out-of-hand by most orthodox scientists. But there have been speculations.

"Remember, it was entirely due to chance that Paul was killed. It was just as likely to have been you instead. Or neither – or both – of you. Even the truck driver and/or the child. And if it *had* been you . . ."

"Then Paul would now be living in our home. Without me. And he might well have written that entry in the diary."

"Yes," Ferguson reluctantly conceded. "This may sound fantastic to you, but . . ."

"Go *on*."

"As you wish. The speculations can be summed up along these lines. There are an infinite number of *possible* futures. None of us knows which one will come to pass, as the Good Book so poetically puts it. This present moment – *our* present moment – is only one of innumerable 'presents' that might have been.

"Therefore, it has been suggested – merely suggested, mind you – that there may be more than one actual present. Why don't we call this other continuum the para-present? It's as good a nonsense-name as any other. That is, one existing simultaneously with 'our' present. Such parallel universes or multiple time-tracks are nothing new in science fiction. They go right back to 'The Plattner Story' – "

"By H. G. Wells. I remember reading it. Years ago, now."

But Ferguson was being carried away by the exuberance of his own verbosity:

"There's a much later story by Murray Leinster which bears a strong resemblance to your own account. I can't recall the title, offhand. It'll come back to me – probably just after you leave! People always talk glibly about truth being stranger than fiction, but I believe that fiction can often influence reality.

"Anyhow, think of the possibilities. Just suppose that Alexander the Great hadn't died at the age of – thirty-two, was it? – but had gone on to conquer the entire ancient world. Or that Adolf Hitler had become a famous painter instead of an infamous dictator. What kind of para-presents would have been created, in each case?

"The possibilities must be infinite – literally speaking. One of my favourite sf novels is *The Guns of the South*, by Harry Turtledove, in which – "

"That's the idea, Diana." Ferguson stemmed the nascent verbal tide. "But I'd prefer to discuss your particular case."

"Fire away, then."

"Before that marble bench actually struck your car windshield, there were at least three main 'presents' in the possible future. One in which you were hit, and one . . . But how do we know that the one in which Paul was hit is the only present? The other, *para*-presents could also have happened and very probably did."

"If all that were true, Paul would be alive in a para-present where it was *me* who'd been killed. As I'm now living in a para-present where *he* had been killed." Diana had been speaking half to herself. Then, directly at Ferguson: "Do you really think that could be the answer?"

"It might – and it might not."

Diana's almost electric-blue eyes shone with new-found hope. "Thanks, John." She stood up, pecked Ferguson on the cheek. "You've been a very great help to me."

"I very much hope so, Diana. I'll see you to the door. Please feel free to call on me again – at any time and for any reason."

Ferguson had the ill-defined look of a man who doesn't know if he's glad or sorry.

Diana's erratic mental state concerned me, of course, but I was caught on the horns of an ethical dilemma. I could (a) have reported her odd behaviour to the proper medical authorities or (b) have allowed nature to take its course. But there was little evidence to prove her clinically insane, let alone a danger to the public weal. I finally decided upon option (b) – the Pontius Pilate approach, if you like.

I did, however, use my contacts in the half-world of advertising to check on Diana's conduct during the next fortnight. While Diana worked conscientiously and talked quite normally in the daytime, only I suspected that she returned home each evening to renew her acquaintance with the impossible. I kept on telling myself that there was no *reason* for such an extraordinary thing to happen to even such an exceptional woman as Diana Weaver.

I didn't meet Diana Weaver again until two weeks after our 'fateful' discussion in my apartment. We met each other, quite by accident, in a quiet downtown coffee bar. I'd never seen her in the Blackthorn before – not that I'm complaining, mind you.

"Good afternoon, Diana." Originality has always been my strongest suit. "Sure, 'tis a fine fresh day we're havin'."

"Long time, no see," Diana said, with one of her old hello-happy-to-see-you smiles. "Sit yourself down, John, and take the weight off your brains."

"Don't you mean feet?"

"No, I do not."

We ordered coffees and exchanged some mumblety-mumblety small talk. Then I asked Diana if she'd undergone any of those . . . experiences . . . during the past fortnight. Well, it seemed like a good idea to me at the time.

"I'm back to my old self, John." Diana was enthusiastic, to say the least of it. "No – I've taken on a *new* self. I no longer have to remind myself that Paul is dead. Now I have clear proof that he *isn't* dead."

I mouthed a few interruptive words, but Diana was in full spate:

"Paul writes to me in his diary, which appears every day on the same desk, at just about the same time. I read his messages, before writing to him in return. The diary only materialized for brief periods at first. But the duration has gradually increased until I've been able to read most of the entries made since Paul's . . . transmigration. His feelings for me are, if anything, stronger than before.

"Then, during the second week, things began to go a bit sour. To know that Paul was alive in some para-present comforted me, but to be hopelessly separated from him has become unendurable. There seems to be no *meaning* in a universe where a woman can only write letters to her husband in another now that only *might* exist."

"So near, and yet so far."

"Exactly!"

We drank some coffee, put our cups back on the table.

"Diana – those snapshots you showed me – may I please borrow them for a while? I'd like to subject them to a more thorough examination. It's not that I – "

"Of course, John." She took the photographs from her handbag and handed them over to me. "I don't actually need them any more."

"Why not?"

"Paul agrees with you. There *is* more than one present. In the para-present I'm in, Paul was killed. In the para-present I'm in, I was killed."

"But it's only a *theory*. For one thing, the – "

"Paul told me something else, by the way," Diana broke ruthlessly in. "I'd almost forgotten about it. Did you have a near-accident the other night?"

I was struck dumb by surprise.

"According to him, somebody almost ran you over in a car while you were jogging on the old Wolf Hill Road."

I finally found my voice: "Yes, I was running along the roadside when a car came out of nowhere – or so it seemed to me – and mounted the grass verge. I had to jump into the bushes to avoid being hit. The obviously drunken driver just raced away. "If I'd been six feet nearer the road . . ."

"Where Paul is now, John, you *were* six feet nearer the road. It was a bad accident – there. You were thrown across the front of the car and hit the ground. The driver – our mutual, alcoholic friend, Fred McKelvey – lost control of the car and crossed into a ditch. He was killed instantly."

"How about the . . . other me?"

"In Paul's para-present, you're lying in hospital, with a broken back."

"I don't believe it!" The Blackthorn was a bit more crowded by this time, and the background noise was getting on my nerves. That's what I like to tell myself, anyway. "
No – I *can't* believe it."

"Your beliefs and disbeliefs are entirely beside the point."

"Diana," I said, trying to calm things down, "can all this be true? And, if so, how can you account for it?"

"Diana and I were – no, *are* – a close couple."

I manfully refrained from saying "The understatement of the decade" or something else to that stupefying effect.

"It was mere chance that separated us," Diana went on. "Now the strong feeling we have for each other is drawing us back together again. There's an old saying about two people becoming 'one flesh'. If such a thing were possible, it would happen to Paul and me.

"After all, perhaps it was only a single pebble or an extra droplet of rain water that made the car swerve just enough to get Paul killed – where I am, that is. A very little thing, whatever it was. So with so much pulling us together – why, sometimes the barrier wears a bit thin."

"'Barrier'? I don't follow you."

"The front gate phenomena was only the beginning," Diana said over my voice, as if she really wasn't hearing me. "Paul often leaves a door closed in the house where he lives – *our* house, only it's in his para-present – while I open the same door where I am. And vice versa, of course."

"That's all very well." I tried hard to sound reasonable. "But is there any future in it for you – or Paul?"

"We're hoping for a breakthrough soon – in one para-present or the other. Paul's diary is sometimes in the para-present where he lives and sometimes in this para-present of mine." Then her voice shook with violent emotion: "If ever I'm in his para-present or he's in mine – even for a moment – all the demons in Hell couldn't part us again."

People were taking an interest in our suddenly heated conversation. "Take it easy, Diana. We've got to think things through, logically. There must be a *reason* behind all this – "

"I'm a little closer to the problem than you are, John." She gave out an almost silent sigh. "But I'll try to be more – what's that word you like? – *rational*. I've been thinking along the lines of transcendental meditation or, perhaps, mind over matter. But the effects interest me much more than the causes – if any."

"There is no such thing as an effect without a cause – even though it might seem to be that way, every now and then."

"That's the major difference between us, John. I'm very well prepared to accept an effect without a cause."

"In other words, you've come to believe in miracles?"

Diana laughed lightly. "If you like . . ."

"Have it your own way, Diana – as per usual."
My voice was a hymn to resignation. "I like to argue
with facts, not opinions." She just shrugged her well-
rounded shoulders, so I added: "I've got to leave now,
but we must get together again soonest."

"And why not?" was the offhand response. "I'll
keep you posted, in any case."

"Don't hesitate to call upon me for help. At any
time of the day – or night."

"Thanks for the dubious offer. Incidentally, these
para-present manifestations may force us to revise all
our notions concerning ghosts and other supernatural
phenomena." Diana sounded perfectly serious, but
there was a mischievious glint in her eyes. "Suppose
that ghosts are really displaced persons in the space-
time continuum – just like Paul and me. Think about it,
you hidebound old sceptic!"

Effective answers came there none, so I muttered
something like "Hmm . . . " The conversation flagged
after a while and we went our separate ways. I picked
up the tab.

Hidebound old sceptic or not, I did think about it,
coming to the sadly inevitable conclusion that Diana
Weaver had crossed that intangible borderline between
sanity and madness. It was, in fact, her third week of
insanity. I managed to piece the story together, as
follows:

Diana had previously regarded work as a haven
from grief, but now she begrudged every moment spent
away from her home. The prospect of missing even a
brief contact with Paul haunted him throughout the
day. He was soon looked upon with a fair degree of
suspicion by her colleagues. Not surprisingly, her
appearances at the office grew ever more infrequent;
they ceased altogether as the 'end game' approached.

No one came warm- or even cold-calling to the Weaver house any more. Mrs. Lunn, the part-time cleaning lady, had been summarily dismissed and Diana's friends soon learned to give her a wide berth. The field had been well and truly cleared for . . . you'll just have to wait and see.

"Grief affects different people in different ways," I told myself. "Caring is a habit that's got to be cultivated. Some people do it and others don't."

You might remember the old story about the man attending his wife's funeral. He breaks down at the church, he breaks down at the cemetery, he sobs uncontrollably all the way home. His best friend, who accompanies him, tries to cheer him up by saying: "It isn't the end of the world. I'll bet that before the year is out you'll meet a new woman, take her out, maybe even marry her."

"I know that," laments the man," but what about *tonight*?"

Bleak and black humour, of course, every time I hear that story, it reminds me of some people I know. The ones who don't seem to care. But Diana Weaver isn't like that. The trouble with *her* is that she cares too damned much.

Closer to psychic home, there was no possible way for Diana Weaver to have found out about that near-accident with Fred McKelvey's car. I hadn't mentioned it to anyone – not even the police – because I'd no idea of who had been driving the car. Unless Diana herself had been behind the steering wheel. But that was sheer paranoia. Wasn't it?

I had to leave my days on an out-of-town assignment for *New Sociologist* magazine. It wasn't a particularly onerous assignment (something to do with an enquiry into inner-city deprivation, of all un-John

Ferguson things). I was able to frequent the Aldebaran Bookshop, which specializes in fantasy and science fiction. And, as luck and/or fate would have it, I picked up a second-hand copy of Murray Leinster's *Twists in Time*.

Or, as both the front cover and spine would have it, 'Six Startling Stories of *Twists in Time*.' The Avon paperback – which actually contained seven stories – had cost 35c in 1960. It cost me considerably more than that, at specialist dealer prices, but I wasn't about to complain. For the fifth story was entitled 'The Other Now' . . .

Leinster has always been an underrated f & sf writer, in my opinion, and 'The Other Now' is one of his better short stories. The no-nonsense writing style was clear to the point of transparency, perhaps a little too clear for most 'literary' critics, but it helped to put across Leinster's central premise – a wry variation on the parallel universe theme.

I was overwhelmingly struck by the resemblances between 'The Other Now' and the story told to me by Diana Weaver. The hero, Jimmy Patterson, had lost his wife, Jane, in much the same way as Diana had lost Paul. The basic situation matched that of its real-life analogue, even if some details were subtly different. I recognized myself in the best-friend character, Haynes. Coincidence, or . . . ?

"'People talk glibly about truth being stranger than fiction, but I believe that fiction can often influence reality . . .'"

My own words returned to prompt me, but they raised more questions that they answered. Although Diana Weaver liked science fiction, I had no way of knowing if she even owned a copy of 'The Other Now', let alone read it. And, if Diana actually was

146

insane, her subconscious mind might have seized upon the parallel universe notion as a compensatory fantasy for the loss of Paul.

'From Homer to Einstein, men have pondered the strange paradoxes of time and wondered, "What if . . . ?"' ran the back-cover blurb. 'Now, from the pyrotechnic pen of a science-fiction virtuoso, here are six (*sic*) dazzling ifs of time guaranteed to spin the hardest head. So read on, until tomorrow . . . or maybe yesterday.'

I *did* read on, during the long train journey home, rediscovering such old Leinster favourites as 'Sam, This is You', and 'The Fourth-Dimensional Demonstrator'. But I avoided reading any more of 'The Other Now': that particular dazzling if had managed to spin one of the world's hardest heads. Or two, if we can count Diana Weaver.

There was a recorded message from Diana waiting for me on my ansaphone:

Beep!

"Hello, John. Why do you bother owning a mobile phone? But forget that. Just listen to my progress report. I told you about my experiments with TM. Well, don't ask me *how* or *why*, but the trance state seems to make me more receptive to . . . you-know-what. It's like the 'John Carter' novels by Edgar Rice Burroughs, in which Our Hero simply *willed* himself to Mars and – hey, presto! – he was there. Extravagant fiction today, cold fact tomorrow. 'Bye for now."

Click!

I was badly shaken. Not only by what Diana had said, but also the ultra-euphoric way in which she had said it. If the hoped-for reunion with Paul did not take place, she could sink into a permanent state of melancholia. Or – on a no less mad but 'happier' level – she might just convince herself that the barrier had broken down. By this time, even my own sanity was hanging in the balance.

Diana's reference to the Barsoomian novels of Edgar Rice Burroughs proved that she'd been thinking along science-fictional lines. My suggestion about the Leinster short story had failed to take or she had made a conscious decision to distance herself from it. And I couldn't help thinking that the transcendental meditation bit was little more than a verbal smokescreen.

Everything about the para-present or other-now mystery was so damned subjective. There had to be some way of independently verifying Diana's story, at least in part, and just such a way came into my mind. I mind a quick (mobile) telephone call before speed-dialling her home number.

"Diana Weaver." She sounded uncharacteristically brusque. "Who is it?"

"It's me – John Ferguson. I finally caught your phone message, though I'm damned if it makes any kind of sense. You told me, last week, that Fred McKelvey was driving the car that almost ran me over?"

"That's right," she snapped back. "So what?"

"You told me that McKelvey was killed, there in Paul's para-present. But, more to the point I'm making, I hadn't told anyone about the incident. Just now I phoned Fred – and it *was* him."

"Really?"

I ignored the disinterest in Diana's voice.

"The near-fatal crash scared the bejasus out of him. He hasn't taken a drink since." My next sentence seems, in retrospect, to have been a bit on the lame side. "I didn't tell him he was dead, though."

"Uncommonly wise of you."

"I'm coming over to your place, right away. We've got to talk this thing out."

"No. I'm sorry, John." Diana's voice was polite but firm. "Paul and I are pretty close to each other, now. We've already touched hands – "

"Impossible!"

"There's no doubt about it. The barrier has worn very thin. It should break soon."

"Please, Diana. Listen to reason. It – the barrier – can't break. It *mustn't* break."

Her reply was an infuriatingly lazy "Oh, yes?"

"Yes!" What would happen if you turned up where Paul is, or if he turned up where you are? The whole fabric of space-time might be torn up. And how could you explain your 'resurrection' – or Paul's – to the authorities?"

"I don't know and I don't care." Diana might as well have been in a trance. There was no sure way of telling. "We'd be together again, no matter how it turned out. That's the only thing that matters to us."

"Pure lunacy! Inertia. Conservation of energy. The Third Law of Thermodynamics. You don't know – "

"But I *do* know, John."

"I say again – impossible!"

"Someone once wrote somewhere that in the sophisticated realm of thinking only the impossible is impossible, by definition, and everything else has a probability factor." Then, all of a synaptic sudden, she seemed to lose interest. "Goodbye, John. Time really is a-wasting."

"No, wait! There's so much more to be discussed." I was desperate to keep her on the etherline. "I've found that story by Murray Lein- "

"One thing more. I tried using a digital camera to record what's been happening, but nothing appears on the memory chip. Don't ask me why – it just doesn't"

I didn't ask her why, but a few mostly untenable theories have since occurred to me.

"Then Paul had one of his brighter ideas. He's been leaving tape-recorded messages for me instead of writing in his diary, as usual. The cassette is right here – on Paul's desk – for your reference in case something should happen. "She paused, for a mere moment. "And something *will* happen."

As Diana finished speaking, I heard an extraneous sound over the telephone. It was a human voice. Only two words across a crackling line, but I swore to myself that it was the voice of Paul Weaver, faint yet triumphant: "Diana! Darling!"

Then Diana slammed down the receiver. "Don't hang up!" came my too-late words. I dialed the number again, but there was no reply.

In next to no time I was driving across town to Diana's suburban home, my mind teeming with theories and counter-theories. "Every psychiatrist knows about patients who write letters to themselves and then – apparently – erase the act of composition from their minds. There's no evidence to support any other interpretation of the facts. Unless . . ." The traffic was light at that hour of the evening; I made the trip in just under ten minutes.

Bloomfield Close showed no overt signs of abnormal happenings; or even normal happenings, if it comes to that. The Weaver house was shrouded in darkness, and I soon gave up my futile pounding against the front door. I was on the point of breaking into the place via one of the shuttered ground floor windows when sanity prevailed at last.

There was nothing else for it but to seek police help. By the time I found the local cop shop, I'd calmed down to a slow simmer.

Very, very carefully, I explained to the professionally phlegmatic desk sergeant that Diana Weaver had been in a highly nervous, if not suicidal state ever since the recent death of her husband. The sergeant, finally won over by my persistence, agreed to send some officers to look over 17 Bloomfield Close.

They had to use a set of skeleton keys in order to enter the house, because every door and window was fastened from the inside. Diana had made certain that nobody could easily interrupt what she and Paul hoped would happen. It soon became obvious that she had left the house. Time for the traditional . . .

AFTERMATH

The police checked out every contingency, from guilty flight to kidnapping. They dragged lakes and combed forests for any signs of Diana Weaver, dead or alive. But she seemed to have vanished into that good old Shakespearean thin air. Nobody ever saw her again; not in *this* world, at any rate.

Several things about the abrupt disappearance of Diana Weaver from our cosmic ken still upset my formerly imperturbable mental balance. The undeniable fact that Diana knew who'd driven the car that had almost killed me on the Wolf Hill Road. The 'double-exposed' photograph of the front gate. And that other snapshot, with its uncannily distinct reproduction of Paul's 'posthumous' diary entry.

However:

If these singular events *did* take place, why did they happen only to Paul and Diana Weaver? What set the whole thing off? Why did these odd happenings begin at that particular time and in that particular manner? Or did anything happen at all? I'd very much like to learn the answers to these, and many other, questions. But I keep my own counsel, or my too-sympathetic family doctor would have me sent away for a lonnnnng rest cure. The same fate that would have overtaken Diana Weaver.

As if all that wasn't enough, there's the book I found on Diana's living room table: *One Hundred Years of Science Fiction* (Simon & Schuster, New York, 1960), edited by Damon Knight. It contains twenty-one great and near-great stories by such Big Names as Arthur C. Clarke and Fritz Leiber. But Part III, OTHER DIMENSIONS, really grabbed my attention. For, along with 'A Subway Named Möbius' (A. J. Deutsch) and 'The Man Who Came Early' (Poul Anderson) is 'The Other Now', by Murray Leinster.

The second-hand book lacks a dust-jacket, the spine is cracked, and the pages are copiously dog-eared. Paul and Diana Weaver were, to my certain knowledge, the kind of reader/collectors who acquired their books either new or Very Good to Fine second-hand. In any case, they had more truck with novels and single-author collections than grab-bag anthologies. This particular volume is little more than a reading copy. And it tends to fall open at the pages reserved for 'The Other Now'. I'm no statistician, but the odds against Diana not having based her story on the Leinster original were lengthening all the time.

My own story, 'Fly Forgotten, As a Dream' (the title has been timely ripped from a line of Isaac Watt's hymn, 'O God, Our Help in Ages Past') has been written using few, if any, direct references to Leinster. But what if Diana had *lived out* the whole thing, in some kind of self-hypnotic trance, after the fatal car accident which so closely resembled its fictional counterpart?

I have here the audio-cassette recording of Paul's voice, which Diana 'bequeathed' to me. It sounds exactly like Paul Weaver, but there is no way of telling whether it was recorded before his death or afterward. The message can be construed in many different ways, and – of course – the recording could be an ingenious fake. Short, sweet, urgent:

Click! "Diana, darling. I miss you terribly. Please come back to me – soon." *Click!*

Leinster might or might not have ended his story there and sent it off for so-many-pence-per-word publication in *Galaxy* magazine. Another job well and gainfully done. But not me, not John Ferguson. Not yet. Maybe not ever.

You know how it often happens in dreams. We find ourselves suddenly transported to the border of a country at once strange and familiar. Nothing on the other side of this paranormal precipice resembles what we know in real life and yet we feel something stir in our memories. We have the near-certainty of having been that way before. Perhaps we have been there in a previous dream – or in a previous life.

The more I think about Paul and Diana Weaver, the more I feel that they're thinking about me. Especially Diana, which is probably just what I *want* to think. I keep hearing her voice at all hours of the day and night. There have been times when urgent beckoning messages appear on my computer screen. But are they really from Diana or have I 'sent' them to

153

myself? I've written this account in-between such electronic manifestations.

After nearly three quiescent weeks, I now seem to be on the edge of a threshold. In psychology, a threshold means a level at which any given stimulus becomes noticeable. Pain threshold. Noise threshold. So on and so forth. At some point we reach what has been called the *indifference threshold* – the level at which a supreme effort seems to be worth making. I've reached that level. Everything looks so new and clean and sparkling. Not here. Over there. Beyond that ever more permeable 'para-present' barrier.

I can't get a certain quotation out of my head, and I can't find it in any reference book or website. The first line reads: "When the dream dies, what of the dreamer?" And the second: "When the dreamer dies, what of the dream?"

DOC BIGGLES DRUMMOND TEMPLAR
- WHEN HE WAS A BOY

> Spiders, men, and Mother Nature make trapdoors.
> This trapdoor was Hers. It was made of air and water, but the springing mechanism was confusion in the mind of the man who had ventured onto it. What seems Up may be Down.

The foregoing wee thinky bit opens *Escape from Loki*[1] : "THE FIRST ALL-NEW DOC SAVAGE NOVEL SINCE 1949!" (front cover blurb). But, as it turns out, J. G. Ballard has got little to worry about. We're soon off and running – no, falling: "Like a young god who had stepped onto a trapdoor, Lieutenant Clark Savage fell from the heavens into hell . . . He had no parachute. The Allied commanders had decreed that parachutes were for sissies.

But the as yet un-Doctorated Clark Savage, Jr. had (merely) been flying upside-down. And, before one can say "Tally ho!", he is firing incendiary bullets at a pesky aerostat (i.e. observation balloon). *Ka-boom!* Then, before one can say "Wizard prang!", he has crashlanded his blown-to-bits-from-under-him Nieuport biplane into a convenient river, swum ashore in his heavy flying togs, made good . . .

Well, that should give you the general idea about *Escape from Loki*. Philip José Farmer (like Lester Dent/"Kenneth Robeson") long, long before him) gleefully follows the advice given to film-makers by Sam Goldwyn): "Start with an earthquake and build up to a climax."

---

[1] By Philip José Farmer. Bantam 'Falcon' book. August 1991. 214 pp. $4.50.

Farmer more or less chose himself for the job. After all, he wrote *Doc Savage: His Apocalyptic Life* (Doubleday, New York, 1973). Archly subtitled . . .*As the Archangel of Technopolis and Exotica/As the Golden-eyed Hero of 181 Supersagas/As the Bronze Knight of the Running Board/Including His Final Battle Against the Forces of Hell Itself.*

Apocalytic Life doesn't quite measure up to Farmer's earlier fictional biography, *Tarzan Alive* (ditto, 1972), perhaps because Doc Savage (Pseud's Corner, here I come!) lacks the mythopoetic resonance of the jungly Lord Greystoke. But some of the "untrue facts" are, er, interesting. For example: Doc's mother was Arronaxe Larsen, daughter of Arronaxe Land (daughter of Ned Land, the thick-headed harpooner from *20,000 Leagues Under the Sea*) and Wolf Larsen, the Nietzschean scholar/sealhunter/psychopath immortalized by Jack London in *The Sea Wolf.*

Not many people (would want to?) know that.

Farmer has written two previous 'real novels' about Doc Savage. For legal reasons, however, he changed Our Hero's name to Doc Caliban. The first novel, *A Feast Unknown* (Essex House, North Hollywood, 1969) is actually the third volume of Farmer's argued-by-some-to-be-pornographic 'Exorcism' trilogy, closely following *Image of the Beast* (ditto, 1968) and *Blown* (ditto, 1969). It chronicles the epic struggle of Doc Caliban and Lord Grandrith (T****n) against some nasty immortals calling themselves the Nine. FOR WHOM IT MAY CONCERN: There is a grudge match between Caliban and Grandrith that can best/worst be described as cockfighting.

Novel Two is the argued-by-none-to-be-pornographic *The Mad Goblin* (1970), which occupied the same Ace Double-package as *Lord of the Trees* (featuring Tar- Lord Grandrith). *The Mad Goblin* was first published in Britain by Sphere Books, 1983, as *Keeper of the Secrets.* Sphere published a single-volume edition of both novels in 1988 (*The Empire of the Nine*).

Escape from Loki is, however, the pure quill. Farmer puts the boyish wonder through his paces before he officially takes up the cudgels in defence of Truth, Justice, and the Amurrican Way. I'm reminded of the following quotation from Milton's *Paradise Lost* (mainly because it was used as an epigraph to *Apocalyptic Life*):

> But first I mean
> To exercise him in the Wilderness;
> There he shall lay down the rudiments
> Of his great warfare, ere I send him forth
> To conquer Sin and Death, the two grand foes . . .

In this case, the Wilderness is the Great War (later demoted to World War I), during which umpteen heroes of popular fiction won their spurs. Captain Hugh 'Bulldog' Drummond found trench warfare too, *too* boring, so he made lone forays through no-man's-land to slit Hunnish throats. There are vague textual suggestions that Simon 'The Saint' Templar joined the Royal Flying Corps, perhaps sharing a squadron with that aeronautical icon, James Bigglesworth.

Captain W(illiam) E(arle) Johns (1893-1968) gave a hectic realism to his early Biggles stories (*Biggles of the Camel Squadron*, *The Rescue Flight*, etc.) that went far beyond using the correct technical jargon and contemporary slang. Biggles might even be described as an *anti*-war hero. His occasional (silent) monologues against the insanity of combat are quite vitriolic for a nominally get-it-done fighting machine.

"It's a dirty job, but somebody's got to do it" is just about the height of his martial fervour.

However, *Escape from Loki* bears the same relationship to yer actual World War I as *The Blue Max*, i.e., little or none. The background detail ("The Ludendorff offensive, launched March 21, had brought the British and the French to their knees . . .") is encyclopaedic, meaning that it was obviously taken from some encyclopedia. It is, at heart, a baptism-by-fire novel in which Clark Savage, Jr. goes from precocious but callow youth to tried-and-tested leader of men. (Women being one of those good ideas that he hasn't tried out yet.)

Farmer doesn't expend many words on physical descriptions of Clark Savage, Jr. – understandably, considering the breakneck pace. But there's always the cover painting, by Steve Assel, which depicts an aureate cross between Arnold Schwarzenegger and Troy Donahue ("Who he?" – ed.), wearing a Balaclava helmet, goggles, utility belt, khaki trews, and – of course – the standard-issue ripped shirt.

Having said that . . . There is an oddly uncomfortable/comfortably odd scene where the now-imprisioned Clark gazes critically into his pocket mirror, which he evidently keeps for just such a purpose:

> . . . His eyes, tawny and gold-flecked in a bright light, {now} looked dark. As dark as his uncertain future. But futures were always unknown, and a man made his own future – to a certain extent.
>
> Were his eyes really funny-looking? Different, yes. Strange, yes. Not, however, the kind to evoke laughter or ridicule in the viewer. Unless that person was sensitive about his own flaws and peculiarities and, hence, liable to mock others. That must be why that apish colonel had made that unkind remark about his eyes.

He shrugged, and he put the mirror back in his pocket. His father had told him that most youths were overly touchy about their appearance. It was part of adolescence. He would grow out of it. Since more was expected of others his age, he would have to mature faster (p. 45).

It's all Krafft-Ebing away. Where did I put my pocket mirror . . . ?

Seriously, though, Clark's 'maturity' and/or chronological age is a matter worth pursuing. In *Apocalyptic Life*, Farmer reveals that the latent superman broke training on 7 April 1917, the day after the U.S.A. had declared war on Germany. Although he wouldn't turn 16 until November that year, he was 6' 1" tall and weighed 190 pounds. His 'mature' appearance, plus some well-faked papers, enabled him to join the fledgling U.S. Army Air Service.

(According to Farmer, Clark was taught how to fly a plane by "the best pilot in the world", Richard Wentworth *alias* the Spider, G8, and the Shadow. But that way lies bewilderment, if not madness.)

Clark had hoped to be in either the 94th or 95th Pursuit Squadrons at Toulon, but Colonel Billy Mitchell (of later court martial fame) assigned him, temporarily, to a French aerial combat unit. Mitchell, in his final interview with Clark, hinted that he Knew More Than He Was Letting On:

"You're young," Mitchell had said. He added, smiling, "Eighteen, I believe."
Did Mitchell know his true age?

"I'm impressed by your record as a flier, an officer, and your perfect French. You may be disappointed because you won't be with your fellow Americans. But this appointment will reward you in the end. Regardless, GHQ, for some unfathomable reason, has ordered you sent there. Good luck. You'll need it" (pp. 12-3).

"Unfathomable reason". Hmm. When Colonel T. E. Lawrence tried to join the R.A.F. as 'Ross' he was interviewed by a recruitment officer named W. E. Johns. (Yes – the very same.) Johns informed his higher-ups about Lawrence of Arabia's questionable career move,but he was told to extract the digit and fill in the necessary forms.

It may be that Clark's yet-to-be-chronicled escape from his "cloistered life and the never-ending study . . . to test his extraordinary abilities against the greatest evil of them all – Germany" (*Apocalyptic Life*) had been psycho-engineered by his father, in collusion with the powers-that-were. Far-fetched? Or just another case of fiction imitating fact? Anyway, the Boy of Bronze ambles through the shambles like Barry Manilow playing Sgt. Rock. He certainly hasn't whipped himself up into an insensate frenzy over *le filthy Boche*.

On the other hand, Clark tells himself (on page 19) that his father was then "exploring deep inside Brazil" and was unaware of the rapid enlistment. But if he *had* been psycho-engineered . . . cue *Twilight Zone* theme music. Moreover, Clark also reflects upon the fact that his ordinarily loving father was, in some ways, "rather detached and quite scientific {and would} be very interested in how his son handled himself as a soldier stranded in enemy territory."

(Which is, surely, carrying scientific detachment to the *n*th degree.)

Clark Savage, Sr. sounds, to me, like a suitable case for treatment. In *Tarzan Alive* and *Apocalyptic Life*, Farmer explains that the old boy was a fugitive from English justice named James Clark Wildman, who had been villainously implicated in an "almost entirely true" Sherlock Holmes story by Dr. John H. Watson (published under his agent's name, A. Conan Doyle): 'The Adventure of the Priory School'.

There'd be little point in my summarizing the convoluted plot (Farmer's, not Doyle's). Suffice it to say that Wildman (renamed Savage – get it? – by those feardies at Street & Smith magazines) decided to pay society back a thousandfold for his crimes. Being well past it himself, he began turning Little Clark into a super-scientific vigilante who would strike terror into the hearts of evil-doers. And, by no means incidentally, help expiate his father's guilt.

It is to Little Clark's credit that, after taking homicidal revenge for the murder of his father (see *The Man of Bronze*[2]), he ". . . doesn't want to go on killing, killing, killing {because} Criminality is a disease" (*Apocalyptic Life*). Hence the "special college in upstate New York", where crooks are turned into model citizens – although I have my doubts about the morality of *that* strong-medicine procedure.

Meanwhile, back at the plot . . .

After the requisite three escape attempts, Clark Savage, Jr. is sent to a supposedly escape-proof POW camp codenamed Loki, which makes Colditz seem like the Elysian Fields. Loki (pronounced *low-key* or *locky*?) is situated near Berchtesgaden. Clark knows this area quite well, having – believe it or not – once climbed the Obersalzberg Mountain that overlooks the town. The wily Teutons have built it inside limestone caves, with a mini-fortress guarding the only entrance/exit.

However, it soon becomes clear that Loki is more than just a tip for intractable Yanks and other, also-ran nationalities. (Even some Russians who should really have been sent home after the recent Treaty of

---

[2] *Doc Savage Magazine*, March 1933. Bantam, New York, October 1964. By 'Kenneth Robeson'/Lester Dent (1904-59).

Brest Litovsk – it says here.) The camp commandant, Baron-Colonel-Doctor von Hessel, is also a keen *Bazillensammler* (bacilli-collector, as if you didn't know) who amuses himself by conducting experiments into the selective dissemination of plague germs.

As luck(?) would have it, Clark has not only met von Hessel on a previous occasion (pp. 49-57), but he'd also overheard his father describing him as ". . . .in the Imperial German Army. But no one seems to know in what branch. He's a rather sinister character, if my informants are to be believed, and you can expect that he'll come up with something both devastating and inhumane if Germany should go to war" (p. 39).

Von Hessel is a kind of Erich von Stalhein (Biggle's arch-enemy) with piles. He could have been played by the late, great Anton Diffring (with or without piles).

The baleful baron has a glib line in sociological chit-chat. Witness his diatribe against the evil industrialists who are fighting to the last drop of everybody else's blood and his contention that democracy is just a beastly swizz (pp. 53-4). Carl Peterson (Drummond's arch-enemy) and Crown Prince Rudolph (Templar's ditto) were also given to such Bolshie ravings, but a good biff to the chin usually shut *them* up.

Clark contents himself by saying, with an optimism worthy of Voltaire's Candide: "I realize that great evils and wrongs stain the shining shield of the world. But I believe that these may be righted someday" (p. 54).

Von Hessel is well aware of the ongoing program to turn Clark into a real-life *Ubermensch* , and he will Stop at Nothing . . . blah, blah.

In my opinion, however, the baron-colonel-doctor fades to invisibility beside his female ally/live-in-lover, Miss Lily Bugov, the former Countess Idivzhopu. Lily lost her wealth and power after the Russian Revolution. But she hasn't lost her Good Looks, as Farmer is quick – even anxious – to point out:

> Her narrow hips became an unusually small waist which supported a swelling rib cage. Above these were breasts gleaming as white as an Icelander baby's skin. The bare shoulders were lovely but broad. They and the large rib cage were needed to support the more than full bosom. Like twin Venuses born from the sea waves, they rose above the low-cut front of her gown (p. 48).

And the rest of her easily meets the European standard for *femme fatales.* Von Hessel explains, somewhat disdainfully, that the ex-countess how uses her sexual desirability to survive in a male-dominated world and regain some measure of power. The brazen, sensible hussy! She *does* have a few skeletons in her past, most of them belonging to uppity peasants. But let those who are without sin . . .

Irma Peterson – sorry, Lily Bugov may not be the chief villain/ess of the peace, but she certainly has a disproportionate effect upon Clark: "Looking at her hips, he was reminded of the rotary {Wankel?} engine of his Nieuport. This image was followed by that of a pendulum, succeeded by a vision of a two-stroke-cycle engine." He can almost hear the hormones "raging inside him" and the roar of blood "hastening to its appointed place."

Clark blushes sweetly, despite the theoretical knowledge (gained from book-learning, experiences with some primitive societies, and his "sojourns" in Paris) that there is no reason for him to feel guilty or ashamed.

163

Clark Savage, Sr. has got a lot to answer for, psychology-wise. In *Apocalyptic Life*, Farmer states that, although Little Clark's education had been planned down to the last detail, the all-male board made no provision for female teachers, servants, or playmates. "And a man who doesn't know woman is half a man. Or half a superman."

Eat your heart out, Sigmund Freud. Funnily(?) enough, Farmer mentions (in *Escape fromLoki*) that the Savages had one attended a few lectures given by Freud, probably on the vexed question of his psychoanalytical theories . Clark muses: "The proof was in the pudding – that is, time would show their validity or invalidity" (p. 138). I wonder if he lived long enough to read H. J. Eysenck's *Decline and Fall of the Freudian Empire* (Viking, London, 1985)?

The plot! The plot!

After some miscellaneous hugger-mugger, Clark leads a revolt of the put-upon POWs. He finally confronts von Hessel, who is really quite decent about the whole thing: "You took me aback for a moment, Lieutenant Clark Savage, Junior, superman-to-be. But I should have guessed that it was you. Who else could have caused all this chaos and destruction and brought about this successful uprising? I underestimated you, my fine American friend" (p. 196).

However, the beastly baron has been playing a deeper game than 'mere' bacteriological warfare. It won't surprise faithful readers of Philip José Farmer to learn that his man preoccupation is achieving immortality, or a reasonable facsimile thereof. He makes Clark an offer he can't accept and the novel ends in the way that all such novels should – indeed, *must* – end.

Perhaps the most likeable/irritating thing about *Escape from Loki* is the way it encourages the Spot-the-Guest Star Syndrome, *à la A Bridge Too Far*. The five aides-to-be of Clark Savage, Jr. make their debuts at irregular intervals. They are, in no particular order: William Harper Littlejohn (Johnny), civilian intelligence officer; Captain Thomas J. Roberts (Long Tom); Lieutenant Colonel Blodgett Mayfair (Monk); Major/later Colonel John Renwick (Renny); Lieutenant Colonel/later Brigadier General Theodore Marley Brooks (Ham).

Farmer hits just the right note in presenting the love-hate-love relationship between Monk and Ham; neither antagonist ever *quite* wins their incessantly waspish war of the words. The other members of the gang also run true to their (future) form, e.g. Johnny uses his verbal trademark, "I'll be superamalgamated!" (p. 106), following it up with: "If any offspring of our anthropoid ancestors, Adam and Eve, can escape from this petrous trap, I'll kiss his glutei maximi. His minimi, too" (*ibid*).

There is an adequate cast of bit-players, including: Zad, von Hessel's ginormous Russkie minder; Colonel Duntreath, the top-ranking POW at Camp Loki; Captain Deauville, a French artilleryman; Murdstone, the archetypal "wee, sleekit, cow'rin, tim'rous beastie"; sundry Huns, unably represented by Sergeant Mixenheimer and Corporal Schuckheider.

Escape from Loki is one of the best sequels by other hands yet written, managing – like Robert Goldsborough's Nero Wolfe pastiches (*Murder in E Minor*, *The Last Coincidence*, etc.) – to embellish the primary source material rather than just rearrange it. Moreover, I'd say that it's the most disciplined novel that Farmer has written since *The Unreasoning Mask*

(Putnam, New York, 1981), perhaps because his all-over-the-place imagination had to be focused in a linear path.[3] He also bungs in some acceptable science fiction (the above-mentioned immortality) and a spot of Dennis Wheatley-type devil worship.

Loki works a whole lot better than George Pal's 1975 movie, *Doc Savage, The Man of Bronze*; starring Ron 'TV Tarzan' Ely. Farmer wrote the screenplay for *The Thousand-Headed Man,* its unproduced sequel.

But I'm not happy about the Western Front being used as an adventure playground. Humphrey Cobb's novel *Paths of Glory* might never have been written, or –especially – filmed (by Stanley Kubrick). I'm even more unhappy about the unequal punishment meted out to the principal unprincipled villains. Baron-Colonel-Doctor von Hessel slips away, bloodied but unbowed. Meanwhile, the admittedly un-darling Lili Bugov is tormented beyond any mere plot necessity; perhaps for the 'crime' of sexual desirability. I ask you: Has Germaine Greer lived in vain?

Python Isle (Bantam 'Falcon', October 1991), the first volume in a new and regrettably short-lived series of Doc Savage adventures, was written by Will Murray under the Kenneth Robeson *alias*. Murry/Robeson based it upon an unpublished yarn that Lester Dent outlined in 1935.

It is to be hoped, however, that Philip José Farmer will at some future time produce follow-ups to *Escape from Loki*, using more biographical material out of *Apocalyptic Life.* For (a mildly paraphrased) example: During the Argonne operation (September – November 1918), Clark Savage, Jr. met one of his

---

[3] Ditto Farmer's 'official' Tarzan ® novel ,*The Dark Heart of Time* (Ballantine/Del Rey, June 1999).

innumerable cousins, Flight Lieutenant John Drummond Clayton (Tarzan, for short), who was temporarily attached to the U.S. Army Air Service.

One cannot choose but wonder. Did Biggles or Simon Templar ever pay Clark a flying visit, with Bulldog Drummond along for the ride? Are these men related, in some way, to the Boy of Bronze? The Reading Public has a Right to Know.

THEY DON'T MAKE CHRISTMAS LIKE
THEY USED TO

It was Christmas morning on Mars, 2150 A.D.

In standard years, of course. Christmas Day on Mars, along with the other humans-inhabited worlds of the Solar System, was timed to coincide with Christmas Day on Old Mother Earth, irrespective of the many diverse interplanetary calendars. All things considered, it was an eminently practical arrangement.

The spacious main room of the Innes household in Clarke City looked like a scene from *A Christmas Carol*. It had been designed that way by the domestic computer. Traditional Christmases were 'in' this year. A synthlog fire blazed merrily away in the pseudo-antique grate, throwing off the occasional hot-looking but environmentally benign spark.

Pride of place was given over to a gaily bedecked Christmas tree. JUST LIKE THE REAL THING USED TO BE!, as the manufacturers so blithely claimed. But the illusion was spoilt by the multi-coloured lazebulbs which festooned its plastic branches. A variable current set these lazebulbs tinkling at random intervals with festive music, everything from 'Rudolph, the Red-Nosed Reindeer' to 'Winter Wonderland'.

Jonathan and Maria Innes were seated at the breakfast table, watching some kind of Christmas extravaganza in the deep video field which shimmered before the opposite wall. The strident music all but drowned out the delicate strains of 'Silent Night' that were now emanating from the lazebulbs.

No self-respecting production of *A Christmas Carol* would be complete without Tiny Tim, and this

168

one was no exception. Eight-year-old Timothy Innes came tiptoeing down the stairs in his stockinged feet. The Dickensian tableau had been the domestic computer's affectionate joke on young master Timothy.

The tow-haired boy hung back from entering the main room. There was a troubled expression on his fresh, fine-featured face. He'd been confined to his room for most of the previous day, having talked back once too often. Uncertainly, he gazed down at his sturdy father and darkly pretty mother.

Jonathan Innes was a geologist – no, Areologist (from the Greek word for Mars). Maria was a mathematician. Unemployment was virtually unknown on Mars. Every able-bodied Martian had a job of some description.

It was Jonathan who spotted him first. He called out in a welcoming voice: "Hello there! Merry Christmas!"

Maria turned, smiled, and followed suit: "Merry Christmas, darling."

"Merry Christmas," Timmy responded, flatly. He couldn't bring himself to look straight at them.

"Your breakfast is under the microgrill," his mother intoned, giving him one of her you-don't-fool-me-for-a-moment looks. "Run along and get it."

"Yes, Mummy."

Timmy went through to the kitchen, switched off the microgrill, and collected his breakfast. It was the time-honoured 'Ulster fry' combination of bacon and eggs, plus soda and potato breads, with what passed for real coffee. For once, however, the artful aromas failed to stimulate his taste buds.

On his way back to the main room, Timmy paused to listen by the swing door. It was a habit he had fallen into, lately. Jonathan was saying:

169

". . . don't understand Timmy. When I was eight years old I got one of those fully functional Planet Hopper models. I nearly wrecked my bedroom with it. Boy, was I ever in trouble over that!"

"Diddums," said Maria, caustically. "I blame that crazy old uncle of yours. He probably gave you that Space Hopper toy, in the first place."

"Abner? What's *he* got to do with it?"

"He's got *everything* to do with it. Filling up the boy's head with all kinds of nonsense."

"If anything, Timmy has become too quiet. Listless, even. It isn't nat- "

"Remember what Abner told us this time last year? 'They don't make Christmas like they used to' – hah! It's a good thing for all concerned that he's been safely put away . . . "

Maria stopped as Timmy chose that moment to clump back into the main room. *Mummy shouldn't talk that way about Uncle Abner. He's the only person who really understands me.*

Timmy could see (great-) Uncle Abner in the iris of his mind's eye. The mental image showed a tall, white-haired man. Aged but not yet old, thanks to longevity treatments. He had wise blue eyes that saw straight through to the secret soul of an over-imaginative boy. Abner Innes was – and would always be – the perfect uncle.

The still-thoughtful boy brought his breakfast over to the table and sat down at his usual place. He merely picked at his food, however, as if by reflex action.

All of a sudden, the scene in the trivid field shifted and changed. There was a burst of attention-grabbing music, then the anchor man said unctuously:

"This is just to remind you, folks, that the next snowfall will start at two o'clock, Greater Martian Time. Courtesy of Weathermakers, Inc. We want all you kiddies out there in Trividland to put down those toys after Christmas dinner. {He pronounced it *X*-mas.} Then go outside and snowfight with each other. And that goes for all you parents as well!"

"Yes" (Jonathan) "No!" (Maria)

"Let's *all* get in on the act, because today is a {cue background crescendo} White Christmas!"

The anchor man's well-scrubbed, almost cherubic face faded from view. It was soon replaced by the opening credit titles of a lately rediscovered classic film: *Santa Claus Conquers the Martians*, starring Pia Zadora. But the Innes family was no longer paying any attention to the trivid field.

"How about it, son?" Jonathan said kindly. "Shall we go out and rip up that snow after dinner?"

"If you like," Timmy replied, with a marked lack of enthusiasm.

"Never mind me, Timmy. How about you? Wouldn't *you* like to snowfight?"

Timmy shook his head, murmuring a dull "No, thank you."

Maria sighed in exasperation but Jonathan remained his usual patient, good-humoured self. "By the way, son, you haven't mentioned your presents."

"They were very . . . nice." Timmy's voice was dangerously close to being spiteful. "Thank you very much, Mummy and Daddy."

"Have you finished assembling your interstellar scout ship?"

"No – not yet."

"Or played your synthesizer? I haven't heard any noises – I mean, music – from it so far."

"No, sir. I'm not int- " Timmy glanced off to one side. "I'm just not in the mood."

"Well, if that's – "

"Timmy!" his mother cut in. "Show a little more respect, if not gratitude."

The sad-eyed boy sat in silence, dourly pretending to finish his breakfast. He personified defiance for its own sake. "Dumb insolence," said Maria.

Jonathan took up the parental inquisition from where his wife had left off: "Are you disappointed, Timmy? Was there something you especially wanted that we didn't get for you?" He smiled wryly. "You don't tell us very much, you know."

"Yes." Timmy looked up at him, sharply. "I would have liked a book!"

"A 'book'?" Jonathan said, quizzically. Then he went on: "Do you mean a real, old-fashioned *printed* book, made with actual paper, not a VR version?"

"That's right. Just like *A Christmas Carol*."

The omnipresent domestic computer, taking its cue from Timmy's last statement, recited: "'Stave One. *Marley's Ghost*. Marley was dead, to begin with. There was no doubt whatever about that. The register of his burial was signed by – '"

Maria proximity-switched the garrulous narrator to silence.

"But I've explained all that to you before, son." Jonathan spoke slowly so as to conceal his mounting irritation. "More times than I can count. It's been *decades* since printed books were made – not since long before you were born."

"It wouldn't have needed to be a *new* book."

"Antique books can hardly be found on Earth nowadays, let alone Mars, and they cost a fortune.

Progress marches on." There was now a brittle edge to Jonathan's voice. "Books can't tell you half the things that the Interplanetary Net can – or even the trivid."

Jonathan flicked his fingers lightly over the trivid prox-control, and the field menu showed the dozen varied programs which were currently available to all subscribers.

"Look, Timmy. There's the new adventure serial: *I Was Pursued by Plutonian Plasmoids.* How about that, now?"

Timmy ignored the trivid field completely. He looked right up into his father's eyes, saying plaintively: "Please tell me, Daddy – what is Christmas?"

"'Christmas'?" Jonathan, though startled, was grateful for any opportunity to communicate with his fretful child. "*Today* is Christmas. It's – well – it's a holiday. People are kind to each other and exchange presents. But I've watched you look it up on the Net."

"Is that all?"

"It should be enough!" His mother's usually calm voice was now verging on the shrill. "It should be *more* than enough that people are friendly and happy."

"But why? The Net didn't tell me that."

Maria started to say something, then changed her mind. She developed a sudden interest in the floor tiles.

"Why winter?" Jonathan laughed, a trifle nervously. "Why spring – or the stars in the sky? They're only words, and words aren't all that important. You should *enjoy* things more, Timmy, and worry less about what they mean."

While Jonathan lapsed into a pensive silence, Maria stood up and walked across to the front window. She gazed out at the grey sky, which was tinged with amber radiance caused by sun-devilled reflections from the distant Argyre desert.

Mars was no longer the starkly inimical planet it had been less than two hundred years ago; thanks to terraforming, the sophisticated technique of making over an alien world so that human beings can live upon it in reasonable comfort. Atmosphere cracking plants, gravity augmentation, hydroponic farming, thermal difference moholes, all that Kim Stanley Robinson stuff. The greening of Mars gained momentum with every five-year Environmental Plan. But there was still plenty of room for improvement.

Clarke City, the Martian capital, was more like an English provincial town than a fully-fledged metropolis. But then, most of its ten thousand or so citizens had never known such Earthy people warrens as New York City or Tokyo. It had been named after the pioneer science-fiction writer, Arthur C. Clarke, whose novel, *The Sands of Mars* (Sidgwick & Jackson, London, 1951), still enjoyed a brisk sale on the Red Planet. In trivid form, of course.

Maria's eyes held a haunted look as she finally spoke:

"You don't realize how lucky you are, Timmy. My grandmother told me that – when she was a little girl, back on Earth – the world suffered from wars, genocidal purges, and . . . troubles of every kind.

"People fighting and killing each other, often for totally irrational reasons. In many parts of that sad world, millions of men, women, and children starved because they had no food. Try to imagine that. The same pattern was repeated here, on Mars, during the Early Days when terraforming was just beginning to take.

"But we 'Martians' soon learned to work together in peace. We had to co-operate – or else! And even Old Mother Earth herself is peaceful, these days. We're living in an altogether different System today. A *better* System."

"Yes, Mummy," said Timmy, trying to avoid her no-laughing-matter gaze . . . *I've heard it all before . . .* "I understand."

Once again, Jonathan came to his conversational rescue: "Well, let's not brood about the bad old days. I suppose you'd like to get back to your presents, Timmy?"

"Yes!" He wanted nothing more than to escape from this fraught situation. "I'd like that. Very much."

"All right, then." Jonathan grinned at Timmy, in a man-to-man fashion. "Go on upstairs and play for a while. After dinner, we'll build ourselves a snow-Martian."

Timmy smiled, non-committally.

"And later on, we can all act out scenes from *A Christmas Carol*," said his mother, with forced gaiety. "You can play at being Tiny Tim."

"'God bless us, every one!'" chirped the still cued-in domestic computer, keeping up the Dickensian charade. Jonathan and Maria laughed, in a thankful release of tension, while Timmy took his dejected leave.

The main room became a welter of rival sounds; twittering domestic computer, melodic lazebulbs, and a clamorous trivid field. Then the computer fell silent once more, and even the trivid decreased in volume – for the time being, at any rate. But the lazebulbs played fitfully on, this time with a crystalline rendition of 'Away in a Manger'.

Upstairs in the snug haven of his room, five minutes later, Timmy pondered over what his parents had told him. He'd thrown the interstellar scout ship model against one wall, the 'music' synthesizer against another, and just about everything else in the place had been artlessly disarranged. But he didn't even look at his personal computer.

The almost-but-not-quite shockproof synthesizer blurted out the odd – sometimes *very* odd – sound, giving the impression that it was being operated by someone with hyperactive but inept fingers. Timmy made the sly decision to leave unwell enough alone.

"They'll think I'm playing, and keep out of my way."

Timmy's tiny robotic playmates, Podkayne and Clark, stayed tactfully inert. But they need not have worried; their pensive human pal was now huddled by the window, looking outwards.

The heat from inside the house misted up the strawberry-hued window panes. Timmy cleared a swathe with his hand and gazed out at the streetscape of suburban Clarke City. Everything was white except for the glistening solar cells on the rooftops, patiently gleaning energy from orbiting satellites. Much the same view could have been observed in any other Martian citylet. It all seemed to be such a far cry from *The Sands of* Mars.

He soon lost interest in the blanched panorama. His mind wandered off elsewhere – anywhere. But the words of Jonathan and Maria Innes never quite went away from him.

It wasn't so much that Timmy didn't believe his parents. He did believe them, but only up to a point. Obviously, people should be nice to each other, on general principles, but there had to be more to Christmas than that.

Uncle Abner could have explained everything to him. Timmy looked at the lone Christmas card on his bedside table. It had been signed by Uncle Abner, all right, but there was no personal message. "Probably against the Workhouse rules," he said, using Abner's truth-in-jest term for the E. J. Stark Rest Home.

Then an inspiration struck Timmy. He almost shouted in his enthusias. "Maybe Uncle Abner left something useful behind him, in his old room." He recalled the title of a juvenile adventure serial: *The Hardy Boys on 61 Cygni C*. "Something that could help me clear up this mystery."

Timmy left his room and stood, stork-like, at the top of the stairs.

There came a burst of increased sound from the trivid field. It was the United Planets anthem, prefacing an hour of comsat-relayed entertainment from every inhabited part of the Solar System. *The Show of the Centuries*, or so it was always called.

Timmy turned and walked quietly along the landing until he reached the door of the room that had once been occupied by his great-uncle Abner. He soon was safely inside what amounted to a stuffy old glory hole.

After Uncle Abner's involuntary departure from the Innes household, there had been a lot of talk about clearing out his former billet. Filling it up, perhaps, as a spare bedroom for any supernumerary guests. Maria was always talking about it, but Jonathan kept putting it off. The bottom line was that Martians didn't throw many elaborate house parties.

According to Jonathan and the old man himself, Abner Innes had been a real jack-of-all-trades during

177

his most active years. Space Marine, shuttle pilot, 'Beltide' asteroid miner, even a minister of the cloth. But a serious groundcar accident, just outside Clarke City, had terminated his chequered career. It had left him crippled in body, but not in spirit.

The smallish room was piled high with what Uncle Abner called footlockers. Also miscellaneous trunks and cases. The intervening spaces were filled up with all manner of objects which had outlasted their utility or value. Timmy had already rummaged through the four large footlockers, marvelling at the 'ancien' clothes and weird artefacts stuffed into them.

"Now I'll look inside that big black trunk." The trunk in question was, indeed, both big and black. It had always filled Timmy with an uncanny trepidation. This time, however, he disengaged the rusty catch and pushed back the creaking lid.

Dust motes swarmed in the otherwise aseptic air, making Timmy cough and rub his eyes. Looking away from the trunk, he caught sight of Uncle Abner's rickety rocking chair, which had been consigned to a dingy corner. It brought back memories . . .

. . . of Uncle Abner teetering back and forth in the perilous seat, while smoking an environmentally hostile 'Meerschaum' pipe. More to the point, however, Timmy recalled his truly great uncle's long talks about the Good/Bad/Indifferent/Old Days. They had been liberally interspersed with advice on how to get along with the worlds in general and parents in particular.

Uncle Abner had lived his long life by the maxim "Don't express an opinion until the reasons supporting that opinion are clear in your own mind." He'd started to explain how Christmas was more than just another holiday when . . ."Why? *Why*?"

Timmy almost threw himself into exploring the old trunk, but some little time elapsed before his watery eyes could fully see the contents. For the most part, it also contained much off-colour clothing and assorted *objets d'art*. Then, underneath all this paraphernalia, he found a book.

The covers of this time-worn volume were missing, and it was badly torn. Many of the foxed pages were loose, or absent altogether. Timmy picked up the book and began reading aloud at random:

"'Sufficient unto the day is the evil thereof'"/"'Judge not according to the appearance, but give righteous judgement'"/"'For what shall it profit a man, if he shall gain the whole world and lose his own soul?'"

And so on and on. Then he happened upon a passage that had been heavily underlined:"'For unto you is born this day in the city of David a Saviour, which is Christ the Lord.'" Timmy read the next verse; silently, this time. From that point forwards, he was hooked. The mostly unfamiliar words seemed to resonate with some dormant part of his mind that had just been quickened into life.

Timmy was still reading, abstractedly, when his mother's soft but acerbic voice translated him back into common reality: "So that's where you are? I might have known it." He turned around so fast that his neck suffered a painful crick.

"We've been looking all over the house for you," Maria went on. "The Christmas dinner is almost ready to be served." Then she took off at a tangent: "Trust Abner to have disconnected the sensors in this room."

"H-hello, Mummy." Timmy was tongue-tied and even slightly afraid. His mind was still roiling with half-understood concepts and the effects of psychic disorientation. He wouldn't have put it quite that way, of course. "I-I'm sorry. I didn't mean to upset . . ."

But Maria wasn't really listening to him. She half-turned in the doorway, averting her head.

"He's here, Jonathan. Sitting in the middle of Abner's old rubbish. *Now* will you agree with me that it ought to be got rid of – PDQ? And you say 'So much to do, so little time' – "

"I suppose you're right, dear," his father said, from the floor below. "I'll get down to it tomorrow morning, first thing." He continued, more cheerfully: "After all, it will be Boxing Day."

"No!" Maria snapped. "I'd rather you did it right away. Our Christmas dinner will just have to wait for a while longer."

"But there's no – "

"Empty all those 'footlocker' things, and the trunks, and the cartons. Put everything degradeable down the disposal. I'll have the garbage technicians call for the rest of it next week."

"Yes, dear," came Jonathan's if-that's-the-way-you-want-it reply. "I'm on my way up."

While this near-monologue was going on, Timmy had been trying to make sense of everything he'd just learned or half-learned. Uncle Abner had once told him that "To travel hopefully is a better thing than to arrive, and the true success is to labour." He also emphasized the importance of asking questions, even if – no, *especially* if –the answers were equivocal and led to other, even more difficult questions.

I don't know . . . Maria took Timmy by the arm, none too gently, and almost jerked him to his feet. "As for you, young man, I'll give you an airbath immediately."

Timmy still held tightly to the unidentified volume as his mother dragged him off to the bathroom. Then Maria (who had been complaining about the damaged synthesizer) suddenly said: "What have you got there?"

"It's a book, Mummy. About Christmas," Timmy said, telling the truth as far as he knew it. He added, diffidently: "Can I keep it?"

"No, you can't. It's *filthy*. I'll throw it into the disposal."

There was a brief, but significant pause. Timmy knew with an overwhelming certainty that he would never lose the most important words; no matter what happened to the book itself. They were *his*, now and for always.

Thank you, Uncle Abner.

He might find another copy of this enigmatic book and meet somebody else who could explain it to him. And – although Uncle Abner wasn't allowed visitors or electronic mail, for 'health reasons' – there was still the off-chance of one last get-together. In any event, he would bide his time and keep asking the next question.

"Here you are." He gently placed the book into his mother's expectant fingers. *It's a book, a very good book. But there'll be plenty of other books. They can't all be lost or destroyed.*

"I'm doing this for your own good, Timmy. I only want what's best for you – always. You'll understand that, all in good time."

Then he smiled a warm smile. Maria's strained face relaxed, and she smiled with him. It made her look years younger. More importantly, his mother seemed to be *happy*.

181

"The people of Mars have lost a lot more than they've gained in this single-minded scrabble after basic survival," Uncle Abner had once told him. "Even hard-working pioneers must spare the time for rest and reflection."

Timmy looked more closely at his mother; really looking at her, as if for the very first time. He thought of many different things to speak to her about, including home-cooked dinners and snowfights. But he finally contented himself with a heartfelt: "Merry, *merry* Christmas, Mummy."

A PRESENCE IN THE SPRING

"It's a beautiful day for a walk."

Heather Maxwell strode blithely along the Serpentine Road. A fitful spray of gentle spring rain played upon her smiling, upturned face. The weather had been whimsical, of late; bright sunshine interspersed with squally showers.

"Julia. My dear little sister. You loved the springtime so much." Her eyes darkened, her voice lost pitch. "It just isn't fair."

Hyde Park was thinly populated at this middling hour of the afternoon. A non-blinking eye in London's perpetual storm.

Heather noticed some old-age pensioners who were solemnly taking their dogs for a walk – or was it the other way round? – and the occasional jogger. A few down-and-outs sat immobile on the park benches, withdrawn into their private thought-words. Afternoon people. "Nowhere to go, nothing to do, nobody to see." She tuned them out of her mind.

Then the air wiped itself into sudden, deep-focus clarity. Heather froze rather than stopped. She saw herself standing on the other side of the path. No mere accidental or deliberate double. Herself. A real out-of-body experience – complete with ectoplasmic Zoomar lens.

"Karshman told me something about random phase effects." Heather's attention, however, soon focussed upon her own solid image across the way. "Tall – but not too tall. Slim – but not too slim. Blue eyes. No – aquamarine." She also took approving stock of the ash-blonde hair that framed a symmetrical face.

But, even as Heather entertained these self-praising thoughts, her viewpoint became medium-shot natural. It was automatic, beyond mere will power. She had no live memory of transitional movement. Then – there. Now – here. In less than the time needed to think about it.

The woman's – *her* – physique still looked taller than average, about five-foot seven in ordinary walking shoes. And a coppery hued poncho did much, but not enough, to hide the fact that she was losing the battle of the bulges. Not out; just started on the down staircase.

Heather was suddenly swept by chilly spindrift from the nearby Boating Lake. She shivered against the unexpected cold. It was almost as if the cold wind had entered her very soul. Images of Julia replaced the phase-effect doppelgänger in a cinematic wipe-dissolve sequence.

"Time heals all wounds. The ultimate cliché. Well, it doesn't work that way. Not for me."

Heather couldn't rid herself of the dreadful certainty that Julia's death had been her fault. In some measure, whether large or small. It was becoming more and more difficult to shake off these recurring bouts of depression. Karshman was very understanding, of good-doctorly course, but he didn't understand – *couldn't* understand.

All of a sudden, Heather felt tired; tired and hungry. The day had been a gruelling one for her, and it wasn't over yet. The Dell Restaurant was close by. She decided to rest there a while, have some roast beef sandwiches washed down with strong tea.

Heather was soon seated at a table in the almost deserted restaurant. The tea was strong and the roast beef sandwiches were more than palatable. She no longer felt tired or hungry, but her mind was still in a turmoil . . .

"Any time you're ready, Miss Maxwell."

"It won't . . . hurt?"

"Of course not . . ."

She forced herself to stare thoughtfully out at the green-brown landscape of Hyde Park. The vaguely pastoral panorama struck another chord in her memory: "I love the countryside. It's so green, and cool, and clean. Julia was safe there. I should never have persuaded her to leave."

'There' was Moreton Pinkney, a snug little village set deep in the rural heartland of Northamptonshire. Ox-Eye Cottage, to be exact. The teenaged Heather Masson had found it altogether too snug, so she'd left it for London at the first opportunity. Metropolitan life suited her, and she eventually became established as a programmer with a multi-national computer firm. She was now financially secure, with a fair-sized apartment in St. John's Wood.

The same no-nonsense philosophy marked her attitude to the opposite sex. Heather accepted men on a take-it-or-leave-it basis. They remained, for the most part, on the edge of her social world. No dominant males need apply. And homesickness had never been a problem. She'd been far too busy for any such wool-gathering. In any case, her parents fitted the description of affectionate but distant.

Heather did keep up a regular e- and snail-mail correspondence with Julia, who had always occupied a special place in her emotional life. She had repeatedly invited her little sister to visit her in London. But Julia gave the impression of being a confirmed stay-at-home girl. Then, one windswept November evening, Julia had appeared on her front doorstep, suitcase in hand.

"Hello, Heather. Surprise, surprise! My, but you're looking well. I've landed myself a job with the Civil Service. The Passport Office, to be precise. Well, aren't you going to ask me in?"

"Of course, Julia," Heather had replied, completely taken aback. "My home is your home."

Heather hadn't set eyes on Julia since she herself had left home, almost three years previously. There had been photographs, of course, but they did not prepare her for the abrupt reality. Her little sister was no longer so little. The 'new' Julia was a fully-grown nineteen year-old girl, slightly shorter than her elder sibling, with a figure that could best be described as pleasantly plump.

Maxwells major and minor had, physically, a great deal in common. They owned the same kind of red-gold hair, worn equally medium-long, and the same shade of green eyes. The general similarity was more striking than the particular differences. But Julia was much more introverted than her outward-bound sister. She was a constant reader; fiction, non-fiction, and – above all – poetry.

Heather recalled a verse from one of Julia's favourite poems, *So We'll Go No More A Roving*, by Lord Byron: "So, we'll go no more a roving/So late into the night/Though the heart be still as loving/And the moon be still as bright."

The poem was a chillingly appropriate one, under the circumstances.

As children, Heather and Julia had been inseparable companions, well-nigh walking the length and breadth of their local countryside. Heather's passion for aimless hiking had waned over the intervening years, but Julia had remained a happy wanderer.

186

"She was begging for trouble!" Heather wrung her hands under the poncho.

The counterman looked worried. Heather smiled at him before ordering another cup of tea. *I've got to pull myself together*, she admonished herself. *Let the dead past bury its dead. As for the future, well . . .*

Julia had never really adapted herself to the mundane realities of urban life. She had, simply speaking, ignored it. To her, London was just another brand-new territory ripe for exploration. Bookshops, libraries, museums, art galleries – all sorts of cultural places.

Heather was glad to see Julia enjoying herself in her own harmless way. Until, that is, she formed the not-so-harmless habit of walking home from the Passport Office in Petty France via a circuitous route which took her through most, if not all, of London's famous royal parks. Hyde Park, especially:

"Rotten Row is far from being rotten! The name probably comes from *Route du Roi* – French for Road of the King. It's actually a sandy track reserved for horse riders. And I love that statue of Rima, by Jacob Epstein, based on the character from W. H. Hudson's novel *Green Mansions*. You *must* have read it. There's also the Serpentine, a big artificial lake built by Queen Caroline, wife of King George the Second . . ."

She might have swallowed a guide book on the subject.

More often than not, Julia wouldn't return to their shared apartment until well after dark. Then she'd eaten, showered, and contentedly settled down in her favourite armchair with a book (sometimes old, sometimes new). Heather had tried to warn her feckless kid sister against roaming alone about the parks at such dangerous hours. But Julia had reacted with uncompromising moral indignation:

"A woman has a *right* to walk in the park."

Julia was to pay a high price for her egalitarian principles – a terribly high price. The foredoomed tragedy had taken place one spring evening in Hyde Park. She'd been hacked to death by some as yet unknown homicidal maniac. It had been Heather's duty, late the following day, to identify the mutilated body of her sister. Everything at the morgue had been so impersonal, with human death and mourning subordinated to a mechanistic standard operating procedure.

Dr. Karshman had waffled on about something called Interactionism, his pet theory of the relation between mind and body. It assumed interaction or – what was it, now? – reciprocal causation between the two, mind acting on body and body on mind. A sound mind in a sound body and vice versa. Easier said than done, old boy.

It was, however, the sheer stupidity of Julia's untimely death that still infuriated Heather: *Julia would still be alive and well today, if only she'd listened to me. Surely that wasn't too much to ask? But she defied me at every turn –*

"A penny for your thoughts."

The soft-spoken, masculine voice jolted Heather out of her reverie. She looked up, convulsively, to find that a young man was now seated across the table-top from her – an unfamiliar and yet recognizable young man.

"I beg your pardon?"

"Oh, it doesn't really matter," the young man said, in what she somehow knew to be his usual self-dismissive conversational tone. He was average; no

188

other word in the English language summed him up better.

Heather just went on looking at him.

"I'm sorry for disturbing you, Miss, Mrs., er, Ms. . . .? My name is Fallon – Rodney Fallon."

"Hello." She pointedly declined the young man's clumsy invitation to call him by name, and she refused to volunteer her own. *If I ignore him, he'll go away soon enough. He might seem to be harmless enough, but you never can tell.*

However, Rodney Fallon seemed determined to strike up some kind of a dialogue with her: "I was taking a walk, then the rain started pouring down. That reminds me of an old film called *A Walk in the Spring Rain*, starring Ingrid Bergman. Have you ever – "

Heather stonewalled him with an inflexible "No." Then she averted her gaze, musing: *All men think with their glands. Major premise: I'm a 'girl'. Minor premise: I'm alone. Conclusion: I'm legitimate 'prey'. The same old sexist syllogism.*

"Well, the rain seems to have thinned out a bit," said Rodney Fallon. He smiled ruefully and rose to his feet. "I'd better be getting along then."

The would-be knight errant beat a hasty, undignified retreat. He hadn't even finished his tea and crumpet.

"Goodbye – and good riddance" came Heather's half-whispered fare thee unwell.

It was now late afternoon. The Dell Restaurant had become crowded with rush hour customers, and everyone seemed to be talking at once. Taped music, from the likes of James Last or Richard Clayderman, added to the din. The counterman shot professional glances in her direction.

Although Heather appeared to be locked into a state of suspended cogitation, she was actually going over what Karshman had said about psycho-physical problems in the cerebral cortex. The walls of the restaurant 'closed in' upon her. She took a deep breath, stood up, and wended her way towards the exit.

"People," she told herself, "there are far too many *people*."

Outside, the westering sun was shining wanly through the gunmetal-grey cloud cover. Spectral semi-darkness now pervaded the parkland. The rain had petered out; for the time being, at any rate.

Heather set off in the direction of Rotten Row. She moved like an automaton. Her mind was elsewhere, and else-when. The 'where' was her apartment in St. John's Wood. The 'when' was that very morning. She was chopping up vegetables with a large kitchen knife . . .

"Any time you're ready, Miss Maxwell." The voice came from some equidistant point in both space and time. Karshman's bass-baritone voice. "It won't . . .hurt?" Her own voice, this time. "Of course not." Karshman again.

The voices didn't so much stop as fade away into imperceptible limbo. There was talk of thought waves, coherent images, monitor screens. Another random phase effect? No matter. She was back chopping vegetables, while a contented half-smile played about her lips. She had slept soundly the previous night, for the first time in weeks.

Soft, early morning music came from the tiny, tiny radio that was close beside her. It was one of the local easy-listening stations. Then the announcer interrupted the melodic *mélange* with a time check: 8:57 A.M.

Heather's smile broadened.

"It's good to be out of that stifling hospital – if only for a little while." Her voice almost sang the words. "Why, I've got the whole day to myself!"

Heather went on with her culinary work. The knife in her right hand moved up and down with machine-like precision. Everything was so peaceful and *safe* here, in her own well-found kitchen. But the nine o'clock news bulletin served to remind her that safety is, after all, only a cruel illusion:

"Early this morning, the dead body of a young woman was discovered by police officers in the grounds of St. James' Park. Police believe this brutal slaying to have been the work of the so-called Royal Parks Ripper, who has claimed six female victims during the past year. The identity – "

Heather hit the off-switch – a little too hard – and the radio spluttered into silence. Then she began to cry, uncontrollably, like an injured child. She stormed her way out of the kitchen and into the living room.

"Is there no end to this nightmare? I need a nice, long walk, to help clear my head."

No time was wasted over elaborate travel preparations. Heather threw on her trusty copper-coloured poncho and entered the aureate outdoor morning. The air was crisp and clean, with a hint of soft spring rain in the near future.

"A woman has a *right* to walk in the park." Heather spoke to the empty street, seeing Julia's outraged face reflected in the rear-view mirror of her mind. Dr. Karshman would have called it a defence reaction, taken to avoid something there is a strong desire to conceal, but she was long past caring about *him*.

Heather went on to mentally retrace her journey through Central London's cafés, department stores, bookshops, museums, art galleries, and sporadic green areas, before she found herself back in the present moment.

Evening was coming up fast. The sun itself had finally vanished from the sky, but the western horizon rioted in red-gold resplendence. A raking wind sprang up, as if from nowhere.

"It's so cold," Heather murmured, shivering like an aspen. Then she added: "But Julia is much, much colder. She'll *always* be cold."

The shadowy glade in which Heather presently stood was heartbreakingly familiar. It had been a twelve-month and a day – as Julia would have been minded to put it – since the . . . attack . . . took place, in this very spot. Reality is real to the person who lives it. There is no such thing as 'virtual' reality. Interactive Therapy, Karshman-style.

Heather seated herself upon a park bench situated half-way between two large silver birch trees. The wooden bench was damp from the rain and faintly mildewed. She began to stare sightlessly at some indeterminate point in space.

Dusk deepened into full night as time wore on, but Heather kept up her solitary vigil. She became a shadow, lost among other shadows that finally became one huge shadow. A quotation from *Julius Caesar* cut through the emotional cat's cradle that entangled her mind : *O judgment thou art fled to brutish beasts,/And men hath lost their reason!*

"Men have always been 'brutish beasts'!" Heather said into the clammy darkness. "Shakespeare was, after all, no better than any other man." She caught her breath before adding: "But too many

192

women fall victim to the smug it-can't-happen-to-me syndrome. Innocents abroad. Just like Julia – "

Some sixth sense made Heather stiffen to attention. She peered warily into the half-light that suffused the glade, to no avail. The sound of footsteps reached her ears – heavy footsteps.

Moments later, a man materialized – wraith-like – directly facing the park bench. Mid-thirties. Swarthy, well-built, wearing a dark suit. Lucid grey eyes. The beam from his flashlight illuminated the hunched figure of Heather Maxwell. He stared down at her, in obvious surprise.

"Good evening, ma'am," he said, with automatic politeness. "I am Detective Sergeant Leeming, C.I.D., and I must ask you to move along. The park is – "

But the sergeant's little set speech was to remain forever unfinished. Heather smiled to herself in the gloom. She didn't hear the mundane words that were spoken by Sergeant Leeming. For all rational purposes, she didn't even see him.

"All-or-none response," droned a voice far from back in her mind. "Full intensity and no grading."

Without warning, Heather's right hand emerged from the concealment of her poncho. Starlight limned the stainless steel blade of a large kitchen knife. She hurled herself like an avenging Fury at the still-unsuspecting sergeant.

The point of the blade tore into Sergeant Leeming's chest, only to be deflected by the breastbone. He staggered away from the clumsily-aimed weapon, which inflicted a bloody but superficial gash before imbedding itself in the lining of his jacket.

Meanwhile, Heather's mind was an acid bath of insensate anger. "I've got to kill him," she gasped, trying to free the knife for another homicidal thrust. "Before he kills me, or some other woman. Julia – "

By this time, however, Sergeant Leeming had recovered from his initial shock. He set about disarming his theoretically weaker opponent, but she was possessed of an all-too-real maniacal strength. Chivalry was a luxury he could not afford, in this grim life-or-death struggle.

Heather finally managed to extricate the blade from Sergeant Leeming's jacket. But before she could initiate another attack, he had immobilized her in the trained grip of his right hand.

The nerve-numbing pain should have made Heather drop the knife, if only by sheer reflex action, but she had become sublimely indifferent to pain. Physical pain, at any rate.

"Julia! The world is a jungle. But you would never listen! I only meant to frighten you with the knife. Why don't *any* of them listen?"

Then Sergeant Leeming did something that he'd never done before, and which he fervently hoped he'd never have to do again. Hitting a woman went against the grain of his character, but needs must when the she-devil drives. He delivered a sharp left hook to the point of Heather's jaw. The bloodstained knife fell from her suddenly inert fingers.

Momentum sent Sergeant Leeming to the ground beside Heather. Two uniformed figures, brandishing flashlights, appeared upon the scene. He heaved himself up on one elbow, favouring his injured left side.

"Ah, yes . . . Constables McKinlay and Judd. I'm so . . . glad . . . you decided to . . . join us."

The new arrivals acted with brisk efficiency. P.C. McKinlay knelt to examine the injured sergeant, while

194

W.P.C. Judd ministered to the still form of Heather Maxwell.

"Well, Sarge, I've stopped the bleeding – for a while," reported P.C. McKinlay, after a stint of first-aiding. "The wound isn't very deep, bit it might need to be stitched up. How does it feel now?"

"It hurts like hell, but no doubt I'll survive." He turned his attention to W.P.C. Judd: "How's the girl?"

"The *woman* has just recovered consciousness, but she seems to be a bit – well – disconnected. If you know what I mean."

"I know exactly what you mean. 'Disconnected' is not too strong a word for it." Sergeant Leeming rose gingerly to his feet. "Keep a close watch on her, Constable Judd – a very *close* watch." He took a ragged breath, then continued: "Excuse me. It's about time that I called up some medical assistance."

"All right, Sergeant Leeming. Just a moment . . . "
"Yes?"

"There's a name, here, in her shoulder-bag. Maxwell – Heather Maxwell."

"Maxwell, eh? That name sounds familiar to me."

"The car's parked just round the corner," said P.C. McKinlay, leading their way out of the glade.

"Thanks," muttered the abstracted sergeant. After a long pause, he added: "The female of the species is more deadly than the male."

"What's that, Sarge?"

"Never mind, lad. It was only a piece of poetry. By Rudyard Kipling."

"I'll take your word for it" (in a whisper).

"But unless I'm very far mistaken, we've caught the Royal Parks Ripper." His voice was wearily triumphant. "No one ever suggested that it could be a girl – I mean, woman. Funny thing, psychology."

Heather opened her eyes before Sergeant Leeming had finished speaking. She didn't see him, however, because he wasn't there. In fact, there wasn't even a 'there' to be seen any more. The next voice she heard was going on about the tension that exists between conscious discipline and subconscious desires.

"Reaction formation . . . explicit sexual metaphors . . .an IT-induced psychic trauma gave birth to your rage."

"A woman has a *right* to walk in the park."

"Of *course* she has, Miss Maxwell. Just let me remove these sensor electrodes . . ."

Heather awoke in what looked for all the world like a high-walled bedroom flooded with early-morning sunlight. The bedclothes were blue-white and the royal blue window blinds contrasted strikingly with the much lighter blue of the walls. There had been the same pervasive blueness in the upstairs bedroom which she'd shared with Julia as a seven year-old girl. It was an incredibly accurate trick of mind, right down to the lattice-work shadows.

Then Heather's vision steadied and objects that had been vague and indefinite stood out with extraordinary sharpness. It was not a room out of the past at all and she felt glad that it wasn't. Her childhood had been a happy one and such memories always filled her with an irreparable sense of loss.

"That was all very interesting, Miss Maxwell."

Dr. Karshman's tenor voice was as familiar to her as the standard-issue consulting room itself. The residual blue glow from the inoperative main monitor screen struck the only odd environmental note.

"Do you have a headache, apparent memory gaps, or any sensation of nausea?"

"No, doctor."

"I'm glad to hear it . . ."

Heather took half-notice of what Karshman was saying while she examined him through lowered eyelashes. The doctor sat in a swivel-chair off to her left. He was short and lean-faced. Radiating crows' feet gave a permanently quizzical look to the skin about his mud-brown eyes. Hairline in fast retreat, with tell-tale pink patches creeping up over a dandruffy skull.

He's let himself go a bit. A woman doctor wouldn't dare to let herself get into that state – not if she wanted to keep her male patients.

". . . better take it easy for a while. Interactive Therapy can take a lot out of you as well as putting a lot in!"

Heather laughed politely before asking: "So I cybered up what *might* happen to Julia, one of these days?"

"Exactly. The IT unit forms a purgative playlet out of the pati- subject's repressed fears and anxieties. Hyper-catharsis, to use a word from my own invented terminology. I've based it upon orthodox catharsis, an idea that goes right back to Aristotle. It's also called abreaction. A suppressed emotion is freed by imaginatively reliving the original traumatic experience. *Hyper*-catharsis takes the process – "

"If the idea was good enough for Aristotle," Heather cut in, "then it's good enough for me!"

It was Karshman's turn to laugh politely.

"That's the spirit, young lady. I'll have to deep-analyse the playlet before coming to any definite conclusions. Raw data can't be taken at its face value, however encouraging. But I was impressed by your creative utilization of perceptual experiences. Both real and synthetic, at the ideational level."

"Thank you, Dr. Karshman." She hid her resentment at the 'young lady' sound-bite. "I always did have a vivid imagination."

"Indeed." Karshman's reflexive frown created a new network of facial wrinkles. "If anything, it might be a little *too* vivid. But I do hope that hyper-catharsis has at the very least alleviated your natural, though ever-more morbid anxiety about Julia's wanderings."

"Perhaps, doctor." Then a faraway look glazed over her eyes. "I wonder. How much of what we call 'reality' is actually out . . . there . . . and how much of it is inside our own heads?"

"I know what you mean. Reality versus un- or irreality. The human psyche is very good at creating free-form illusions that have all the force of material truth. Headspace, not cyberspace. More psycho-physics than parapsychology. But there is such a thing as *objective* – "

Heather felt herself phase-shifting away from herself once again. It didn't seem to be a random effect, this time, beyond her conscious control. The room shimmered into hectic clarity. Karshman's voice was neither here nor there; the sound waves came from another space that co-existed with another time. She knew her own mind, and not just in a metaphorical sense.

"The playlet should have had a different ending," Heather heard herself say. "A better ending."

"It isn't a question of endings, Miss Maxwell. Good or bad, happy or sad. The IT unit can offer you a new beginning – *beginnings*, rather.

"I'll make my own new beginnings, if you don't mind," snapped Heather, showing her delayed-action pique at Karshman's 'young lady' remark. *And my own endings*, she told herself. *I made a terribly stupid*

198

mistake. It wasn't Julia who should have been killed, or any other woman. But it really is never too late to learn.

"Do you like going to the theatre, Dr. Karshman – or may I call you Harold?"

"Well, Miss Maxwell – Heather – my close friends know me as Harry. And, yes, I *do* like going to the theatre – unlike any of my ex-wives." There was an embarrassed and embarrassing five-second silence before he limped home with: "Drama is, after all, the purest form of Aristotelian catharsis."

Heather smiled.

"There's an abridged version of *The Canterbury Tales* being performed at the Open Air Theatre in Regent's Park. I think it's called *The Smiler with the Knife*. What do you think . . . Harry?"

EUROPE IS ROOM ENOUGH

The opinions expressed in this story are not (necessarily) those of the author. Any resemblance to real persons, living or dead, is purely fortuitous.

"Attention! Attention!" That stentorian announcement cut through the Euroglais that babbled in Sharon Hazlett's headphones. "Security Drill. Plan B3/791/XG6. All staff members below the rank of Administrator will evacuate the building. Immediately!"

Sharon was a secretary/grade C3 employed in Brussels (the capital city of Brave Little Belgium) at the huge Berlaymont 31/2/aka Madhouse building. She took off the headphones, trying not to snag them in her long, strawberry-blonde hair. "Ouch!"

Trying to assuage the familiar pain, Sharon automatically read off what she had just keyed: "The total amount agreed upon was 8.5 thousand million Euros from the EIB's own resources. The EU's offer . . ."

Snap out of it! came the imperative thought-form. Sharon stood up to her full tall-and-willowy height. She did a quick twirl – "Whee!" – then left the office. "Time's a wasting. Now where did I get *that* one from?"

Sharon took justifiable pride in her academic CV and general knowledge. After all, she had reached this El Dorado/Rainbow's End/European Commission via highly competitive examinations and interviews. Many people aspired, but those who were chosen comprised a tiny percentage of those hopefuls who tried for European Union (EU, for short) employment, and failed. There were usually no second chances.

"Everybody tells me that I should privileged for being a Eurocrat." She frowned, making a slight 'V' mark on her otherwise smooth forehead. "And so I bloody well do!"

Sharon didn't bother re-reading her Handy Guide to Plan B3/791/XG6. She already knew it by mind, if not by heart. During the past few weeks, Plan B3 etc. had been implemented frequently. Sometimes it was restricted to staff members of Administrator rank and above. Sometimes, as now, only junior personnel took part in the fake Exodus.

The Security Drill announcement was made over and over again; in robotic English, French, German, Italian, Dutch, Spanish, Russian, Portuguese, Danish, Hungarian, Irish, Latvian, Finnish ,and many other languages. "I wonder if it's the new Euroglot computer they've just installed on the twenty-third floor. The *whole* twenty-third floor."

Sharon sidled her way into the conga of Other Ranks that was wending its orderly way towards the nearest down staircase. The lifts had been deactivated, for the duration. There was little conversation above the whisper level, and no one moved faster than the standard EU walking pace. "Dignity, always dignity."

For the next too-many minutes, Sharon avoided watching the dandruffy male head directly in front of her. She gazed fixedly at the left-hand wall. It was unrelievedly blank, painted a 'restful' pea green. EU scientists had done considerable research on human colour senses.

Then she saw right into the office of *Herr* Otto Irgendwaz. The portly *chef d'unite* was lying supine upon what looked to her like a psychiatrist's couch, only different. "Talk about being the worse for drink.

Yet another liquid lunch-hour. *Lowenbräu uber alles*. I don't know how he gets aw- "

Sharon's censorious reverie was interrupted when her part of the impromptu procession finally reached the staircase. Once the initial jostling had settled back into the customary slow march, she found herself thinking about the present geopolitical pot-pourri.

The European Union had emerged from the *fin de siècle* Yahoo Years in fine fettle. United, prosperous, and able to run roughshod over all competitors. Every country in the Mighty Continent^{TM} had now joined this commodious community. Switzerland, Turkey, the Balkan and Balkan states, Russia (up to the Urals), Israel, etc. Apart from anything else, it made necessary a fortnight-long Eurovision Song Contest final. For convenience, however, the blue flag showed only twelve yellow state-signifying stars.

Johan Galtung's seminal 1973 book, *The European Community* (as it was then called)*: A Superpower in the Making* had long since been overtaken by the events it predicted. Unlike many another writer on this vexed subject, Galtung took adequate time to explain basic facts, pose/work out political problems, and – above all – to think. The American point of view was well-put in *The United States of Europe* (2004), by T. R. Reid.

Multilungual wall-stickers proclaiming EUROPE IS ROOM ENOUGH reminded Sharon that the EU was more protectionist than ever before. Many outsider nations, from the U.S.A. and Brazil to Russia(beyond the Urals) and China, took umbrage at Europe's new-found strength. Some of them, driven by economic desperation, had even applied to join the EU.

"Turning it into the Elongated Union?"

But the EU powers-that-were remained adamant in their opposition to any further member-state expansion. (Except for the largely unmanned Eurobases on the Moon, Mars, and some of the Jovian satellites.) Now the twin piques of economic disadvantage and political envy had turned the Rest of the World against Fortress Europa.

Galtung had written: "Today the European Community is on the way up. {But, in the furious future} each point of interference will constitute an argument for military strength, for internal security, for a *European* posture towards the East, for the possibility of rapid action in the South. And as the repressive machinery grows, so will the counterwaves."

By that time, the corncrake Security Drill announcement had been replaced with more EUphonious Muzak (something not too unlike Mozart's *Eine Kleine Nachtmusik*). It was oppressively soothing . . . soothing . . . soothing . . .

Sharon couldn't take the threat of an air-strike from some nation-or-nations all that seriously. "There's been talk about a new Eurobuster secret weapon in development at Caltech. Smart bombs, quantum psychics, designer drugs, stuff like that. But then, there's always talk about everything."

She was worried, however, about the nuclear-powered central heating system that had recently been built into the improved Berlaymont. Radiation hazard signs plastered the stairwell to the underground reactor, despite assurances from Official Experts that leaks and/or meltdowns only happened in last-century movies like *The China Syndrome*.

"What was that terrible place in the old Soviet Union called?" Sharon fought against the soporific Muzak, with limited success. "Ah, yes – Chernobyl.

Atomic pile-up. A fallout over some two-headed chickens. Near Kiev. But wasn't it only a novel, by some Polish writer called Frederik?"

In the foolishness of time, Sharon's group joined the main congregation on the *rez-de-chausée*. Everyone faced the wide-open front doors, which were flanked by Atomium-and-Sun emblemed EU Security Guards. "They always look like robots to me. For all I know, they might even *be* robots."

They put Sharon in mind of the real Atomium, a 103-metre high structure built in the shape of a crystalline atom for the 1958 World Trade Fair held in Brussels. This huge stressed-metal 'molecule' was now the mobile headquarters of Europol; it stalked the land like a Martian Fighting Machine from *The War of the Worlds*.

Plan B3/791/XG6 was then completed with typical EU efficiency. Once outside the Berlaymont 31/2, Sharon watched with a fair degree of puzzlement as Administrator types from the Council, Parliament, and other nearby establishments filed into the building. "More robots?" she asked herself, irreverently.

There was a nip in the spring air that seemed almost electrical. Sharon ended up milling about with countless middle/lower EUers and sundry civilians on the far side of Rond-Point Schuman. Nobody spoke, except to themselves. They were all being herded even further away from the Berlaymont 31/2 by Belgian military policemen, GATTling guns held at the ready.

"When things calm down, I'll grab a bite to eat," Sharon promised herself. Even more cheerfully: "And drink! Let me see, now. Maureen O'Hara's? The Brendan Behan. Or that new place – the Split Crow? They've got Ma Caffrey's Dragon Breath ale, on tap."

She gave a great deal of thought to the problem. Until:

Metallic *clacks* and dull *thuds* drew her errant attention back to the Berlaymont 31/2. The new black security blinds, all of them, had been closed simultaneously. One, two, three explosions went off, renting the no longer still air. A thick dust-cloud swirled upwards from pulverized paving stones. There was an insubstantial, opalescent haze immediately surrounding the now windowless structure.

A suitably eerie silence fell over the entire Europolitan area. It was so profound that Sharon could hear the workings of her genuine imitation Timex wrist-watch. *Tick-tock, tick-tock, tick-*

Before the next *tock* could be heard, the Berlaymont 31/2 gave one last gigantic shudder and took off. Up, up, *up* into the mild grey yonder. Unoffending clouds were pushed roughly aside to make way for this literal skyscraper. There was only the most faint of shock waves, but the onlookers suffered more than a thousand psychic traumas.

"Plan B3/791/XG6," said the seemingly novocained Sharon Hazlett. "All those renovations . . . Euroglot computer . . . nuclear-powered central heating system. . . weird couches." Then: "What *else* can possibly happen?"

She didn't have long to wait. *Boom-bang-a-bang!* sounded the first – but not the last – hyperspatial neutron bomb. And the lights went out, all over Common Europe.

In this Euroverse the Long Night had fallen; the shadows were deepening over a populace that would not know another EU Directive. But elsewhere the Yellow Stars and the light of Union lingered; and along the path it once had followed, Euromanity would one day go again.

205

WITCH HAZEL

PROLOGUE

The year is 1757. Ingrid Pitt has just become England's first Secretary of State. Colin Clive conquers Bengal for the Irish East India Company. Sir Walter Scott visits London, where he sees David Garrick in *As You Lick It*.

Britain and France are disputing the ownership of the large island (area: 5,657 km^2) which lies to the north-east of Canada: Ile St. John. Or, as the British prefer to call it, St. John's Island. The Macmic Indians know the place as *Minagoo* (i.e. the Island) and, more poetically, *Abegweit* ('cradled on the waves').

Today, however, it is Canada's smallest province – Prince Edward Island. Red soil. Azure skies. Lush vegetation about neat farmhouses. Sweeping beaches washed by Northumberland Strait and the Gulf of St. Lawrence. *Anne of the Seven Green Gables* performed at the Charlottetown Festival.

1

"It's been an exhausting trip for these homesteaders," Mel Cameron told himself. He surveyed the rough encampment that held some two hundred people and eleven wagons. Concern tightened his already too-thin mouth. "But we've got to keep putting a long distance between ourselves and those Native Americans who burned down the settlement."

For going on eight hours, now, Cameron had scouted the impromptu wagon train's route along the narrow forest trails, which were lined with silver birch and maple trees. Some of the older folk were beginning the show the ill-effects of their arduous trek. Even his own lean, well-tempered body ached in protest, but fatigue was an unaffordable luxury.

Although Cameron would have preferred to carry on regardless, he felt obliged to heed the advice of –

"Lost in thought, Mel?" James Sanderson, M.D. hove into view. "Shame on you. I could've been a French patrol. Or one more pesky Amerindian war party."

"Point taken, Doc." Cameron did little to hide his pique at having been caught out by the hefty sawbones. "Though you're making as much noise as both mobs combined – plus a platoon of redcoats."

Doc Sanderson made no attempt at feigning lordly indifference.

"Redcoats be damned! The Brits have their hands full elsewhere. We can't expect any help from that quarter. Not until we reach Port La Joye. If . . ."

"Hold your horses." Cameron experimented with a smile. "What seems to be the problem?"

"There's no 'seems to be' about it! I've told you before. We haven't enough wagon space for everyone to ride."

"So?"

"So have you seen any witch hazel shrubs around here? I can boil some bark and leaves. The walking wounded can bathe their sore muscles in the tannin extract."

"Sure. Night will be falling soon – and the cold. More to the point, some of these people have taken root." It didn't take long for Cameron's practised gaze to locate the required shrubs. He waved a hand towards them. "Over there, Doc. Help yourself."

"Thanks – I will."

Cameron followed Doc Sanderson across the glade to the area of undergrowth where the witch hazel bloomed. He admired the honey-yellow, spidery flowers that lent blazing colour to the mid-September forest. The petals were already curling up for the long night. Most of the leaves had already fallen off, during the past week or so.

"I can recognize witch hazel," said Cameron, half to himself, while Doc Sanderson harvested what was left of the oval, wavy-toothed leaves. "But I don't know much about it."

"*Hamamelis virginiana*," came the automatic response. "North American variety, at any rate. Grows in slightly acid, moisture-retentive soil. Down to minus 35° centigrade. Four-part calyx. A corolla of four long, narrow petals. Eight stamens. Two pistils."

Cameron groaned. He'd forgotten that the Good Doctor was a walking reference library. Ask him the time of day, and be lectured on celestial mechanics.

"And just look at those nuts – "

"I can only see *one* nut around here."

"No marks for observation." Doc Sanderson was immune to sarcasm, when he was in this abstracted state of mind. "They're uncommonly large. Some kind of mutation, perhaps. Mutations are – "

Cameron readied himself for the pedantic worst. It was not to be, however:

"But forget mutations, for the moment. Here's a real funny wonder. I remember keeping some witch hazel nuts on my surgery desk. One sweltering hot night, I heard snapping noises. Then the sound of hard objects hitting the floor." Doc Sanderson paused for effect. Cameron half-yawned, for much the same reason. "The nut-capsules had burst elastically and cast their seeds all over the place."

"How about the *healing* properties of witch hazel?"

"Oh, yes." Doc Sanderson began scraping bark off the delicate stems. "People have known about witch hazel's medicinal value since . . . well, time out of mind. It's now used in many tried-and-tested astringent drugs. As for more general applications . . "

Cameron winced in anticipation.

"Witch hazel forms the basis of several cosmetics. Ask your mother. The forked branches can be used as divining rods in the search for water and minerals. Possibly arising from its evocative name, which should really be spelt w-y-c-h hazel. After the wych-elm, the leaves – "

"A-*hem*."

"'His hall rofe was full of bacon flythes,/The chamber charged as with wyches/Full of egges, butter, and cheese.'"

Having delivered these poetic exit lines, Doc Sanderson loped off to distill the witch hazel cuttings. Cameron watched his retreated back with a mixture of doubt, relief, and appreciation.

"Good old half-crazy Doc. Every hour's delay can mean added danger. Indisputable fact. But what's the sense of reaching Port La Joye if half the party has been left to die by the wayside."

2

By the time first light had tinted the eastern skyline a golden red, the party was – according to Doc Sanderson – sufficiently recovered to push on towards Port La Joye. Nevertheless, it was quite a while before the horses were fed, wagons checked, and rowdy children brought under control.

209

There was a musty feel to the early-morning air, which was enlivened by intermittent birdsong. A few obstinate stars still tarried in the sky, but even they were soon snuffed out by the steadily waxing sunlight. The bitter night frost had long since evaporated.

Breakfast was eaten in a stony, apprehensive silence. Until, that is, Doc Sanderson started to regale Cameron with further facts and fancies about witch hazel. Doc's learned discourse was punctuated by some dry chuckles and a lot more groans from the captive audience of homesteaders.

Cameron took it stoically enough. After all, he reflected, Doc's witch hazel lotion had been a sovereign remedy for locked muscles and tender skin.

In any case, Cameron had other – more urgent – things on his mind. He looked around at the homesteaders. They were of all ages and physical condition. Mostly Scots-Irish in origin, with a sprinkling of Dutch, German, and Swedish. Even some Frenchies.

"Babes in the wood," he said, under his breath. "My babes. My responsibility."

No sooner had Cameron finished his rabbit stew than he rose up in a single movement. Doc Sanderson was a trifle less agile, but not far behind him. The rest of the breakfast party followed suit.

"Mister Boyd!" The grizzled old wagon master of that name looked expectantly at Cameron, who went on: "Move the wagons up to that clearing I told you about. Make it before noon. I'll meet you there, after scouting the woods ahead."

Mike Boyd grunted something that might have been "Yes." He was a man of few-or-no words.

3

Cameron soon outdistanced the lumbering caravan. He was riding along one of the innumerable forest trails, hemmed in by tree boles and autumn-struck vegetation.

The harried homesteaders were seldom out of his mind. He had sent a few picked men to flank the wagon train, while an experienced Indian fighter brought up the rear. Nothing else could reasonably have been done. But that didn't stop him from dwelling upon unreasonable second thoughts.

Cameron's keen sight and hearing – also his 'sixth sense' – told him that no hostiles stalked this part of the forest. The monotony was getting him down. Then he spotted some witch hazel shrubs, with their petals wide open to catch the available light.

"How did Doc put it?" Cameron ransacked his memory. "'Does the sudden appearance of witch hazel in the autumn woods remind us that, in the midst of death, we are in life?'" He smiled, wryly. "Something like that."

Cameron was so intent upon recalling Doc Sanderson's philosophical musings that he didn't immediately notice an abrupt excess of light. It seemed to come from everywhere at once. Then the glare made him close his eyes, protectively. The horse whinnied in fear.

"What the – " Cameron fought to pacify his skittish mount, barely holding on to the reins. "Easy, boy – easy!"

The light grew in brilliance – and heat – for about five seconds. Then it began to fade. Cameron's re-opened eyes could make out a circular object hanging just above the tree-tops, or so he thought. The disc gleamed yellow, like witch hazel blooms, and the air surrounding it seemed to have been bleached white.

As if burning itself out, the apparition waned to near-invisibility. The central disc became more bronze than yellow and it lost size second by second. Cameron was reminded of an ancient Greek shield, burnished to mirror-like reflectivity. He felt *watched*. A familiar experience for any frontiersman, but this time for no obvious reason.

The sky went calm. As did Cameron's horse. But peace of mind eluded the still-blinking scout.

"I've heard about these . . . fireball . . . things. Been all over the shop, lately." Even as Cameron spoke, the disc winked completely out of existence. "Whoever said they were a Froggie secret weapon doesn't know cow-pats from wild honey. Doc calls them unidentified frying objects – UFOs, for short."

Cameron shook his head, removing immaterial cobwebs.

"But I'd put my money on ball lightning. That is, if I had any money."

Urging his horse forward, Cameron looked up at the cloudless sky and tried to reconcile that tranquil firmament with electrical storms. He was no scholar, but some hard-learned lines from *A Midautumn's Night's Dream* came niggling back at him:

"'. . . as imagination bodies forth/The forms of things unknown, the poet's pen/Turns them to shapes, and gives to airy nothing/A local habitation and a name.'"

But all thoughts of Wilbur Spearshake fled from Cameron's mind less than fifteen minutes later.

4

The watery sun was approaching its zenith when Cameron galloped his horse into the prearranged meeting place. He reined up right beside Doc

Sanderson, then half-slid/hell-fell from the saddle. A quick-minded boy led his horse away to the nearby stream.

"The Devil take it, Doc!" He was trying to stem his anger, without noticeable success. "If we hadn't stopped last evening – well, water under the bridge. There's a small army of Frenchmen waiting ahead of us. Armed to the teeth."

Cameron couldn't help recalling how he'd almost ridden straight into a French patrol. Luckily for him, the soldiers had been complacent to the point of imbecility. He had doubled back, thinking hard all the way.

". . . sick people *always* come first," Doc Sanderson was saying. "But this is no time for lollygagging. Braves on one side of us, Frenchmen on the other." He grimaced. "Looks like we're caught in the jaws of a human vice."

Cameron paused for a much-needed breath. Then: We've got to break through. And, in my opinion, we stand a better chance against the regular soldiers."

Doc Sanderson framed a reply, but Cameron was now speaking to the wagon master:

"Mister Boyd, at three o'clock please take the wagons in that direction." He pointed north-westwards. "Follow the trail I've blazed to a wide clearing. It's the ideal spot for an ambush."

Cameron waved down the angry protests.

"Make sure you arrive there near sunset. After the Froggies attack – which they will – I want you to return their fire. But go easy on the ammunition. We don't have an inexhaustible supply. Bear this point in mind. Manoeuvre the French soldiers so that they're between you and me, but closer to me."

"Hold it, Cameron." Mike Boyd made what might have been the longest speech of his life so far. "Aren't you going with us?"

"No. I'll ride ahead, to take up a position about two hundred metres due east of the clearing. Remember that – it's vital."

Mike Boyd nodded, then went back to his wagon.

"But, Mel," objected Doc Sanderson, "they'll know we haven't got the firepower to beat them off. Nothing remotely like it."

"That," said Cameron, with a light laugh, "is what I hope they'll think."

5

At three o'clock precisely, Mike Boyd signalled for the wagon train to move out. Tired-looking men and women walked beside each overloaded vehicle. The rumble of iron-rimmed wheels mingled with jangling harness, while the reddish dust churned up by this rough passage lingered long in the chilly air.

The caravan of displaced homesteaders made camp at the picked clearing just as twilight was turning into dusk. Fires were lit, more for heat than light. Mike Boyd set about organizing a carefully slanted defensive perimeter. Doc Sanderson prepared to treat the inevitable casualties.

Meanwhile, Cameron had awakened from a well-deserved sleep. His equally tired horse was tethered some distance away.

He had curled up under some bushes, after making sure that the French officers were deploying their forces in accordance with his plan. The only snag had been a daymare about a witch hazel leaf turning into an unidentified frying object, accompanied by manic laughter from Doc Sanderson. And the irrational sensation of being watched returned to haunt him.

"Any moment now," he said, over a yawn. "The conditions are perfect."

Sure enough, the sounds of combat were not long in reaching his ears. Musket fire rattled through the near-night atmosphere. Shouted orders, given in French and English, rose above this martial din.

Cameron moved into action. The day before, Doc Sanderson had shown him the ripe witch hazel capsules and reminisced about their explosive potential. He'd found many more of the mutant-type shrubs during his ride back to the wagon train. Enter the classic simplicity of all great thinking.

Now, seeing the vague shapes of French soldiers moving about in the brush, Cameron grabbed a stick and ran through the witch hazels, striking out at them. One by one, the impacted capsules burst open with the *crack* of a musket shot. Seeds were shot almost forty metres in all directions.

"*Nom de petit chien!*" Cameron heard a frightened French officer exclaim. He translated the man's next words as follows: "We have been outflanked by a superior force of redcoats. Withdraw – before it is too late!"

EPILOGUE

"I guess we can push on to Port La Joye without any further trouble," Cameron told the homesteaders, at a council of peace held early the following day. He added, merrily: "And, Doc, that witch hazel may have soothed our limbs, but it sure as hell irritated those Frenchmen."

PUBLISHER'S NOTE. Every detail in this scholarly monograph has been verified by the Hubble Time-Scope.

EVENTIDE

"'Sunset and evening star, and one clear call for me!'"

Mrs. Sarah Braddock softly quoted Tennyson to herself as she contemplated the fall of dusk on what was the latest in a long line of placid autumn evenings. The darkling scene had, to her wearily-wise eyes, a strange quality of timelessness. This part of England had never seemed to be more English.

Another fragment of poetry, this time by John Keats, fell from her suitably reverent lips: "'Season of mists and mellow fruitfulness. Close bosom-friend of the maturing sun . . .'" Then she lapsed into a meditative silence.

The second-hand paperback she had been reading slid to her lap, folded open at a particular title page. It was *The Infinite Moment*, an American 'Ballantine' book which had somehow turned up at the church jumble sale. (Or flea market, as people said nowadays.) The name John Wyndham had caught her attention, she having borrowed his entertaining fantasias from the once-a-week mobile library.

She couldn't seem to stop herself from buying the slim short-story collection. The idea of a moment having infinite duration might have set some mental wheels in motion. Or was it just the attractive power of popular fiction?

Never mind. Poetry had long been her secret weapon against a world that could be harsh and uncaring. Even, all too often these days, deliberately hostile. The Romantic poets, of course. Nothing modern, experimental, or ("Heaven forbid!") significant. Tennyson and Keats, yes, plus many others

– including Scott, Byron, Shelley, and Browning (both 'versions').

An errant breeze rippled the grey surface of the nearby lake into a flurry of scudding cat's-paws. The wind, when it came off the lake, was bitterly cold. Mrs. Braddock wrapped the thick plaid shawl she was wearing more snugly about her frail old body.

Across the shadow-dappled lawn, the ancient ash tree stood exactly as it had – seemingly – always stood. Its russet-leaved branches had, of course, grown longer with the passing years.

There seemed to be no other houses for miles around. The picture-postcard village of Midthorp wasn't, in fact, all that far away, but it was well-hidden by rolling hills and dense woodland. Only sporadic birdsong and restless insects disturbed the serenity, here.

Mrs. Braddock gazed raptly over her small domain, falling in love with it all over again. She had loved this neat little freehold during her girlhood years. But, somehow, she loved it even more now, in the soft-hued twilight of her life.

A girl named Sarah Lucille Gilchrist had been born in this white-walled bungalow. She had grown up in it, came back to it after her parents and husband had passed away, become old in it.

"Nor," Mrs. Braddock mused, "will I be altogether sorry to shuffle off this mortal coil. I've become a stranger in a terribly strange land."

All of a sudden, she felt her eyelids drop.

The tranquillity of the autumnal evening lulled her into a lanquid *malaise*, wafting her back sixty-odd years to just such an evening when she had sat on this very porch. She had been waiting with an awful ache in her heart for Peter Mitchell, a young arts student at the nearby Shires College.

But Peter had never arrived.

The world about Mrs. Braddock took on an almost hallucinatory vividness, as glimpsed through her half-closed eyes. It seemed as though she were reliving one of her dreams from the far past.

Close by, but out of sight from where she was sitting, there came the measured tread of footsteps on the gravel path. The crunching sound began quite abruptly. It wasn't long before a man, or – rather – a youth, emerged from around the corner into Mrs. Braddock's field of vision. She felt a sudden, sharp tug at ". . . my heartstrings?"

The young man was attired in a blue-black rugby club blazer and fawn cavalry twill slacks. There was a silk scarf tied negligently around his neck, and – tilted rakishly back off his high forehead – a straw hat with a dark-coloured band.

Mrs. Braddock tried hard not to think, about anything at all. But other impressions, mostly unidentifiable, forced themselves upon her attention. The gravel-crunching returned, slightly fainter than before.

"I've got to cheer myself up," she heard someone say, in a barely audible whisper. "Everything is working out for the best."

Then, about ten seconds later, came an outburst of baritone-voiced song. "Roamin' in the gloamin', on the bonny banks o' Clyde – "

The voice and the footsteps came to a simultaneous halt. There was a deep intake of breath, followed by an attenuated silence. The birds and the insects were no longer to be heard. Even the breeze seemed to be locked into a state of suspended animation.

Mrs. Braddock recollected the tune. More to the point, however, she could also identify the voice.

"Moonshine," she admonished herself.

'Moonshine' or not, everything else in that pocket universe was so totally *real*. The arms of her chair felt quite solid beneath her clutching fingers.

Once again the gravel was crunched underfoot, only this time the tread was shifting, uncertain. A bewildered, oh-so-familiar voice said: "My word, that's strange! What's going on?"

Mrs. Braddock's eyes were now very wide open, and unusually clear-sighted. The young man gazed intently at the old lady in the chair, and then past her into the illuminated living room beyond.

"What the – "

A hardbound book slipped from his trembling fingers and thudded on to the path. He attempted to retrieve the fallen book, take off his straw hat, and salvage his dignity all at the same time – with mixed results.

Mrs. Braddock smiled, indulgently. When the young man had pulled himself together, he regarded her with interrogative eyes.

"Don't you recognize me, Peter?" Mrs. Braddock asked, in a melancholy voice which the young man obviously took for disappointment.

"No, ma'am," he admitted, "but you must be Sarah's – Miss Gilchrist's, I should say – grandmother."

She looked at him steadily for some little time before replying. "No, Peter, I am not Sarah's grandmother."

He shook his head in perplexity.

"It's all so *different*," he said distractedly. "Have I come to the wrong house?"

He surveyed the twilit garden before shaking his head once again.

"No, that isn't it. But then, what *has* happened? Please – just *how* do you know me?"

"We have met before, Peter, a long time ago." Then, mindful of the young man's increasing distress, Mrs. Braddock went on: "But you're looking so unwell! Draw up that chair and rest for a while."

"Thank you, Mrs. . . . Braddock," he said, frowning slightly as he tried to identify the name.

She watched him walk away, then return with the chair. Every movement, every line of his tall, lithe body was achingly familiar to her. He sat down and remained silent, staring pensively across the darkening landscape.

Mrs. Braddock passed a hand over her forehead, which was filmed with perspiration. She had never felt so tired . . .

"After I'd recovered from the shock," Peter was saying, "I walked on along the footpath until I reached the turn-off for Woodvale, here. And then, just as I was approaching the corner of the house, everything went . . . weird."

"'Weird'?" Mrs. Braddock prompted him. "What do you mean, Peter?"

"The whole world, I can only suppose. The sun seemed to leap about in the sky, and it wasn't quite as strong. The old ash tree over there suddenly looked bigger."

He glanced off to one side, skittishly.

"And this room – it *is* the same room. But I've never seen the people in those photographs above the mantelpiece. Or that glass-eyed . . . contraption . . . in the corner."

"'Contraption', Peter?" Momentarily puzzled, Mrs. Braddock turned around in her chair and looked back into the living room. Then she said, liltingly: "Why, that's just a television set!"

"'Television set'?" Peter murmured. It was more of a vague statement than a direct question.

Mrs. Braddock laughed, dismissively.

"Yes – or TV, for short. It's like a radio – *wireless*, rather – with pictures. Here, let me show you."

The remote control device lay on the little wickerwork table beside her. She brought the TV set back into electronic life, changing channels rapidly. All the usual piffle (in her wilfully biased opinion) flashed sequentially upon the screen. A sketchy current affairs programme, an inane sitcom, a snooker tournament, and what looked like *The Saint in London*, starring George Sanders.

Mrs. Braddock switched off the TV set no more than two minutes later. The sudden silence surrounded them like an invisible shroud.

"You've been to the cinema, haven't you, Peter?" she said, feeling that some explanation was called for. "Well, a TV set brings the cinema into the privacy of one's own home, complete with sound and colour."

"Yes, ma'am, I have been to the cinema," Peter affirmed dubiously. "Tinted films are old hat, by now, and I've read that all-talking pictures might soon be upon us. But this is like something out of H. G. Wells or that old Frenchman – Jules Verne. What does it all *mean*?"

Mrs. Braddock didn't know what was happening to her and/or Peter Mitchell, if this . . . apparition . .

222

really was Peter Mitchell. But she felt no fear, only a mounting puzzlement. The young man was staring right at her, impolitely, as if he were willing her to answer his question.

"There's an explanation for everything, Peter, if one looks long enough and hard enough."

Peter's temper, which he had somehow managed to hold in check until that moment, started to flare up.

"Then what the deuce – "

He broke off abruptly, listening, his head turned slightly to one side. The insidious sound grew until it filled the air. A relentless mechanical drone, *whicker-whicker-whicker*.

"What's that infernal racket?" Peter asked, anxiously.

Mrs. Braddock gripped his arm, tightly. "It's all right, Peter," she assured him, with forced levity. "Believe you me."

The Lynx helicopter passed right overhead, at little more than tree-top height, heading for the nearby Ravenhill Army base. Its spidery fuselage was silhouetted starkly against the sunset-glow of the western sky, then the baleful machine dropped out of sight and hearing.

Meanwhile, Mrs. Braddock's garden had gradually been turned into a crazy quiltwork of light and shadow. It was fixed in the kind of autumn evening where sunset colours linger and cast a ruddy glimmer over the crepuscular landscape.

"It's just a helicopter, Peter," the old lady informed him. A kind of aeroplane, if you like. Nothing for you to worry about."

"'Helicopter'?" The word didn't seem to belong on his faltering tongue. "But I've *seen* an aeroplane, and *heard* one. That shape . . . that noise . . . it was terrible!"

Mrs. Braddock was finding it more and more difficult to collect her thoughts into a coherent pattern. Peter's image kept shifting in and out of focus, superimposed upon a solid natural backdrop.

"How can I break the truth to him?" she asked herself. "There just doesn't seem to be an easy way out."

Peter interrupted her reverie. "Sarah promised to be here, at this time. Please tell me, Mrs. Braddock – where is she?"

Mrs. Braddock looked kindly at him, but she could think of nothing to say except "Sarah is close by."

"I must find her!" Peter rose to his feet. "She'll be able to tell me what's happening around here!"

She laid a gently restraining hand upon his arm.

"Try to relax, Peter. And tell me about whatever it is that seems to have 'happened'."

"All . . . this." Peter waved expansively. "It's so different, and yet so similar." Then he ran for conversational cover: "I was coming here to return a book which I'd borrowed from Sarah's father – *An Experiment With Time*, by J. W. Dunne."

"Yes, I've read it." Her voice dropped to a whisper. "So long ago."

Peter held the book out for her inspection. "Well, I was actually coming to see Miss Gilchrist." He looked more than a little sheepish. "There's something important I've been meaning to ask her."

"Oh, Peter . . ."

"Anyway, everything was all right until just after I'd narrowly avoided being hit by a falling branch." He shuddered at what to him was a recent bad memory. "Missed me by inches. It's lucky I wasn't killed."

Mrs. Braddock had read about hearts skipping a beat, but this time she felt it happen. If only it *had* happened that way, she told herself, in a fast-running stream of consciousness. 'If' – the most cruel word in the English language.

Although it's odd how things turn out. Most maxims are lies, or at best misleading. Watched kettles do boil, and rolling stones can gather moss. A second chance does sometimes present itself, especially to the person who is ready and willing to accept it.

If Peter Mitchell had, in fact, arrived at Woodvale that long-ago evening, Mrs. Braddock-to-be would almost certainly have married him. In the fullness of time. And then her grown-up children would never have existed. She might still have had children, of course, but they would not have been Leonard and Sylvia.

She had, naturally enough, been angry and hurt.

However, the anger and the hurt changed to grief the very next morning, when she learned that Peter had met with an improbable accident the previous evening. He had been struck down by a falling tree branch whilst walking along the lakeside footpath. Death, according to the coroner's inquest, had been instantaneous, and foul play was not suspected.

Ten seconds either way and Peter would have survived the incident unscathed. Dame Fortune had turned her face away from Peter Mitchell, and – by extension – Sarah Gilchrist.

"It was all so *unfair*." (Peter blinked at the emphatic last word.) A few years later, she had married a rising young architect named Donald Braddock, and the memory of her painful first love receded into oblivion. Or so it had seemed, until this evening of evenings.

But was this merely an hallucination, a quirk of her mind superimposing Peter's face upon a different young man with the same Christian name? And was she hearing things that she wanted to hear?

She looked more closely at him. No, that 'explanation' simply would not do. Straw hats were not often worn by young men, nowadays, and he was wearing Peter's distinctive rugby club blazer. The voice was unmistakable. Without a doubt, he *was* Peter Mitchell.

Many times in the past, Mrs. Braddock had displayed signs of so-called paranormal abilities. Nothing spectacular. Just a knack for finding lost objects, knowing things without having to be told about them, and an occasional 'sixth sense' where personal danger was concerned. Something of a hit-and-miss affair, really.

But it had never before manifested itself in so concentrated a form.

Another possibility stole into her mind. She had once read, somewhere, that ghosts usually haunt the living with a fixed purpose. Jealousy, remorse, pity. Strong affection, equally strong hatred. The whole gamut of human emotions can provide a motive force haunting any person, family, or place.

Mrs. Braddock thought for a few moments, then shook her head. Perhaps – but which one of them was the ghost?

"Peter," she said at last, diffidently.

"Yes?"

"Tell me, Peter – what day is this?"

"'Day'?" he said, shooting her a quizzical glance. "Why, it's Thursday. It's the – let me see, now – the thirtieth of September."

"But the year, Peter, what is the year?"

The young man kept his brown eyes locked on her as he replied. "It's nineteen twenty-seven, of course."

Mrs. Braddock's gaze switched back to the garden. Night had finally fallen. The electric light from the living room was much stronger now, casting its harsh radiance well out over the porch area. Twilight had, indeed, given this part of the world its poetical last gleaming.

"Nineteen twenty-seven," she half-said/half-thought. "Yes – that was the year, and it had been a Thursday. It might very well have been the thirtieth of September . . ."

Peter's tremulous voice recalled Mrs. Braddock to the here and now:

"Why – why did you ask me about the year? That's the odd thing that's happened, isn't it? Somehow, it isn't nineteen twenty-seven any longer. The way the ash tree grew, that . . . helicopter . . . thing. Where am I? *When* am I?"

"I've got something rather important to show you, Peter."

Mrs. Braddock's diary, which she always entered up last thing at night, lay upon the little wickerwork table. She held the still-blank page reserved for that day towards Peter. His eyes grew even more apprehensive as he accepted it.

"Tuesday, the third of October," Peter read, in a speaking-clock monotone. "That's funny. I could have sworn . . ."

"The year is printed at the top of the page."

Pause, then: "Nineteen . . . nineteen eighty-nine!"

The diary fell, unheeded, to the parquet floor.

Peter fought a rearguard action, more in hope than in any real anger. "No! It isn't possible! You're Mrs. Braddock – that's who you said you were. You can't be . . . Sarah."

But then, leaning closer, he managed to distinguish the familiar piquant features of Miss Sarah Lucille Gilchrist in the emaciated face of this old lady who called herself Mrs. Braddock. The likeness was beyond any penumbra of doubt.

"Oh, my God – Sarah!" He buried his face in his hands.

Mrs. Braddock's pale grey eyes misted over with tears, and she closed them for a few moments. When they opened once more, she had regained her composure. In fact, she had never before experienced such a sensation of restfulness.

The doors of perception seemed to lose several hinges at once. For all temporal and spacial purposes, Sarah Braddock and Peter Mitchell were now the only two sentient beings in a pocket universe that extended no further than the front porch. Ever-decreasing energy circles spiralled in upon them.

Mrs. Braddock had the sudden silly notion that she was looking into a darkly reflective camera lens, at right-way-round images of herself and Peter. "More moonshine. Lenses don't work like that – or do they?" A meaningless trick of the waning light, perhaps.

"'Grow old along with me. The best is yet to be.'"

"It's too late for that, Sarah, much too late." Peter's voice was little more than a moan, but the name Sarah rang out loud and clear. "We never had the chance to grow old together. *I* never even had the chance to grow old."

Peter knelt down on the floor, directly in front of her. She could see a big darkness just behind him. It got closer all the accelerated time. "Infinite momentum" she said, with no real understanding.

Mrs. Braddock's fragile, blue-veined hands reached out for the downcast head of Peter Mitchell. She stroked his wayward brown hair, ever so gently. It was like a benediction. The young man started to sob, uncontrollably.

Early next morning, the dead body of Sarah Lucille Braddock was found by her daughter, Sylvia Russell. She had apparently passed away in her sleep, still seated upon the porch. The French windows were wide open, and the lights in the living room had been left on all night.

Sylvia felt her grief tempered by the fact that her mother looked like a woman who had made peace with the world and accepted the inevitability of death. Then she noticed some unusual reading material on the old lady's lap.

"The Infinite Moment," by John Wyndham. "Where did *that* come from, I wonder?" She glanced with automatic curiosity at a laid-open title page. "'Stitch in Time' . . ."

IRISH ENOUGH…?

SCENE: Just outside Ballybutton, a village in the dead centre of Ireland.

Alien spacecraft cuts an emerald aisle through grassy field. CAPTAIN AARG KETH emerges and makes telepathic contact with TERRY NURE, a passing native.

AARG KETH: Greetings, Earthman.

TERRY NURE: You must be meaning *Erse*man.

AARG KETH: I'm sorry. (*He goes straight to the point:*) Can you direct me to the Capital City?

TERRY NURE: I would if I could. (*His eyes twinkle with an age-old devilment.*) But you can't get there from here.

AARG KETH (*confused*): I'll try again somewhere else, then.

AARG KETH *hovers his way back to the spacecraft.* TERRY NURE *waves after him.*

TERRY NURE (*cheerfully*): Good luck to you, sir.

AARG KETH: And the same to you, Erseman Nure.

The spacecraft takes off. It hangs about, uncertainly, for a few minutes. Then – with a WHOOSH! of displaced air molecules – it zooms right back into space.

TERRY NURE (*shaking his head*): Bloody immigrants!

CURTAIN

Lightning Source UK Ltd.
Milton Keynes UK
UKOW03f2035010414

229239UK00001B/2/P